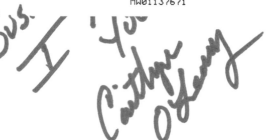

Her Adoring SEAL

Midnight Delta Series

Book Three

By Caitlyn O'Leary

Edited by Lynne St. James

Cover by Valerie Tibbs

Her Adoring SEAL

HIDING IN FEAR

Beth Hildago feels shattered after the time she spent in the hands of the Mexican drug cartel. Now her life is on the line as corrupt authorities try to hunt her down.

FIERCE PROTECTOR

Jack Preston is a decorated Navy SEAL whose family's Texas Ranch is the perfect place for Beth to hide.

ON THE RUN

When Beth's cover is blown, she is once again forced to run. This time Jack is not going to leave her side. But what happens when there is an enemy no one ever expected? Can he keep her safe?

Dedication

To all of our men and women who have served.

Chapter One

They were going to kill her. Jack gripped his gun as he looked into the storage room. Griff was across the square in the bell tower, and Jack had just gotten word he found three of the other doctors and could take down their captors. Aiden and Dex were on other floors of the hospital looking for hostages and tangos. Their lieutenant was outside ready to give the command to Aiden to start taking out the targets. That left him in the basement to find this horror.

The woman was on her knees, her shirt torn, breasts spilling out, and a face covered in blood and bruises. She had one arm wrapped around a man's hips like a lover, her cheek pressed against his thigh, and her blonde hair tangled with his pubic hair. That's where the farce ended. The tip of the knife she held was pressed against his balls, and Jack could see a trickle of blood.

"Come closer and I will cut off his cock," she said in raspy Spanish.

"Kill her." The man commanded to the three other men in the room.

"Sir, the bullet could hit you."

6

"You're two feet away. You can't shoot straight? Kill the bitch!"

The woman flinched, and the knife bit into the man's tender flesh. He yowled.

"Kill her now, she's cutting me."

"You keep talking and threatening me and you'll never father a child. Tell them to back off."

Jack admired her bravery, but what did she think she was going to accomplish? How in the hell did she think she was going to get out of this mess?

He backed away. He couldn't start shooting now because it would endanger the other doctors. They needed a coordinated effort.

He sent a quick text saying he needed a "Go" and fast or they were going to lose a hostage.

His lieutenant replied with 'two minutes.'

"Just walk up and put a gun to her head, you dumb ass," the leader said to one of the men.

Fuck!

He'd have to walk in and not shoot for two minutes.

Jack sauntered into the room.

"I wouldn't do that. Drop your weapons or I'll kill you all." All three men wore the exact same uniforms from the penitentiary where they had escaped after the earthquake. Their weapons were guns they probably stolen from the armory there. They eyed Jack's automatic weapon with trepidation.

"Don't do it. There are three of you and just one of him!" the leader screamed.

"Don't forget her." Jack tipped his head at Carys Adam's, the American doctor they had been sent to rescue. "She seems to be on my side, and she has your leader by the balls." He heard her choked laughter.

"Shoot him!"

"I'm supposed to take you in, and return you to the warden. Otherwise, you'd be dead. Now drop your weapons." The men hesitated.

"Shoot him!"

A shot rang from upstairs.

Thank Fuck!

He unloaded his gun on the three assholes. Hearing a shriek, he turned his head and saw a spray of blood as the leader's groin was sliced open.

Jack rushed to the doctor. She was on the floor, underneath the bloody mess of a soon to be dead man.

8

"Dr. Adams, are you all right?" She didn't answer. "Carys?"

"I killed him? Did I kill him? I didn't mean to." She started to shiver. Jack used what was left of her shirt to wipe away the blood and saw the cut on her chest. He tapped the radio on his wrist.

"Aiden, you done?"

"Affirmative. All tangos down."

"Get to the basement. Dr. Adams is injured."

"Roger."

Their whole SEAL team had been sent to Las Flores after the earthquake because of Dr. Carys Adams, the American doctor from Doctors Without Borders, who had been taken hostage.

"I'm Senior Chief Aiden O'Malley ma'am, the team medic," Aiden said as he got to the storage room and rushed to her side.

"Team?"

"We're Navy SEALs. We're going to get you patched up so we can get you home."

She turned to Jack. "Are you a SEAL too?"

"Yes, ma'am."

9

"Thank you. You saved my life."

"It looks to me like you were well on your way to saving yourself."

****

By the time he got home, he was worn out. His team had stayed in Las Flores for three long weeks, helping to track down and capture the remaining escaped convicts. It wasn't the normal duty for American SEALs, but their lieutenant had made quite a convincing argument to the brass to help the locals.

Unlike most of his teammates, who lived near the Pacific Ocean, Jack lived more on the inland side of San Diego. He liked the dry rolling hills during summer, it reminded him of the part of Texas where he was born and raised. When he opened the door to his condo, he was hit by a wave of heat and went straight to the thermostat. Jack breathed a sigh of relief as the air conditioning kicked in. Going to the kitchen, he filled a pitcher of water and headed to the cactus and succulent garden near his sliding glass door. They were still doing well despite his absence. Obviously Mrs. Marsh had checked in on his plants. After watering them, he finally did what he'd been longing to do.

A trail of clothes marked his path to the bathroom in the master bedroom. He grimaced as he looked in the mirror. He'd lost weight, and he didn't want to jump on the scale. He needed to take leave and go home. A week of Rosa's cooking should put him back in fighting trim.

God, the shower felt like heaven. He stayed in the spray until the water ran cold. He got out and dried off thinking about sinking into the comfort of his own bed when he realized how keyed up he was. He pulled on some shorts and went to the kitchen. He grabbed a Shiner Bock beer from the refrigerator and took it onto the deck. Now that he was refreshed from the shower, the heat felt good as he sat in the lounge chair. Looking off into the horizon, he let images of Las Flores wash over him.

He'd always been good, exceptional even, at compartmentalizing things. But it had been tougher this last trip. He thought about the convicts he'd captured, and in some cases been forced to kill, and he realized it didn't bother him. Taking out the "trash" was something that made him feel worthwhile.

What was making it hard to sleep was thinking of the pain and suffering of the locals. Seventy percent of them were without homes after the devastation of the earthquake. Thousands of people lost their lives in the original quake and hundreds more in the aftershocks. He'd had two nightmares about the bodies being bulldozed into the mass grave. Then there was the shanty town the locals built for themselves. At night when his team should have

11

been getting shut-eye, they'd been helping put up roofs. If you could call the pieces of tin a roof.

Where there was power it was off of generators, so mostly there wasn't power. Forget running water. Instead, there were kids running around barefoot in raw sewage. The aid trucks with food were bombarded each time they showed up, and after they had been sucked dry, there were still hundreds who left empty-handed.

The first call he had made when he had got stateside was to his stepfather, Richard. He knew the man had a lot of pull with many people and charities. He'd told them how devastated the city was. Richard hadn't peppered him with stupid questions. He'd just said he'd take care of it, and Jack knew he would do whatever he possibly could, which would probably include a sizeable donation of his own. That's just the way Richard Preston operated.

It had been the same way when he had taken Jack into his home all those years ago and adopted him. Jack had been a belligerent little shit, but Richard had seen through to the scared little boy and had loved and accepted him. It was years later that Jack had learned Richard had paid his real father a lot of money to give up all parental rights so that he could adopt him. That was Richard, he made obstacles go away.

Jack took a final pull off his beer and thought about getting another one. God, he loved Shiner, it always reminded him of home. He decided against a second. He'd be in San Antonio tomorrow, and he wanted his next Texas beer with fajitas made by Rosa. He hadn't told his mother he was taking leave. He wanted to surprise her, and he couldn't wait to see her expression. God, He missed her. Jack went inside and fell into bed, grateful that he didn't need to set the alarm.

Chapter Two

"Jack!"

There was the smile he'd been hoping for. God, his mother was beautiful. She had the same white blonde hair and blue eyes he did, but on her it looked good. She gripped her cane and started to get up from her spot on the couch.

"Stay there. I'm coming to you."

"Posh, I can get up to hug my son."

Eight steps later he was across the great room and helping his mom up and had her wrapped her in a gentle bear hug. Despite her petite size and the cane, she felt sturdy. Healthy. Like Mom. He breathed her in and felt safe and happy. He blinked rapidly.

"Baby boy. You're home safe and sound. I love you so much."

"Love you more." He kissed her cheek.

"Jack, you look tired. Sit down beside me, and tell me what you can. I know you've been in Las Flores. Richard already started gathering donations and put Margaret Lester on setting up a benefit in San

14

Antonio. She has the Marriott booked near the Riverwalk, and she's already sold half the tickets."

Jack shuddered as he discreetly helped his mom settle back down on the sofa. "That woman scares me."

Grace Preston looked around, pretending someone might overhear, and then leaned in and said, "She's scared me for years. I don't know how your father does it. But he has her eating out of the palm of his hand."

"Don't lie to me mom. She'd do anything you asked and you know it."

"Only because I'm Richard's wife."

Jack shook his head. As much as people loved his dad, you could double it for his mom. They were a power couple in San Antonio society. Considering where she and Jack started in life, it was saying something.

"Honey, why don't you go tell Rosa you're here. You know she loves you, and she's definitely going to want to cook your favorites. You look like you could use some good meals under your belt."

"Fajitas?" he asked hopefully.

"I'm sure she'll make anything you ask for."

He gave her another kiss and squeezed her hand.

"You stay put. I'll be right back."

"My hip isn't bothering me today."

"I'm here to lean on, so use me while I'm here."

"How long do we have you?"

"I'm here for a week." He loved the grin that crossed his mother's face. It made her blue eyes sparkle.

"That's wonderful, Jack. Okay, go see Rosa and come right back."

****

It tickled him to be back with the family. He'd spent part of the afternoon in the kitchen with Rosa, basically getting in the way as she tried to cook. It was an old routine they had going. He would pretend to help, but actually filch food, and she would pretend to be annoyed and give him bites to taste.

"We've missed you, Jack. You should come home more often."

He snagged a piece of cornbread, and she handed him some honey butter to put on it.

"With food like this, it's a wonder I ever left."

"Your mother misses you." Jack shot Rosa a hard look.

"No, nothing like that. She's fine. That man of hers thinks the sun rises and sets on her head. She worries when she watches the news. We all worry, even your brother, David."

Jack thought about his stepbrother and grinned. It had taken awhile for them to come to terms when they first started living together, but now David was his best friend outside of his teammates.

"How is Julia?" Jack asked with a sly grin.

"How can he not see her for the cat she is? It's been over a year and he still hasn't realized she wants him for his money and position."

"He hasn't proposed yet has he?"

"No. I'm hoping she shows her hand before he does." Jack made a mental note to talk to David and see where his head was at.

"Are he and Dad going to be home tonight?"

"Just your dad."

"I better go get ready for dinner." He gave Rosa a quick hug and went in search of his mom. As he reached the great room, he checked his phone and saw he'd received two calls from a San Diego number he didn't recognize. He called back and was soon standing against the wall listening to his commander.

"This is strictly volunteer and you can turn this down. I know you're on leave. Hell, this isn't even your own team." Jack rarely talked to Captain Ivers. Most of his orders came from Lieutenant Jeffries.

"But you're saying they asked for me, and it would be a personal favor to Captain Osterman? Would you like me to do this, Sir?"

"Yes. I wouldn't be asking otherwise," came the decisive reply.

"Where do you need me and when?" Jack didn't want to cut short his leave, but if this was important enough for Ivers to be calling, he wanted to help.

"Lieutenant Gault will be calling you shortly. He heads the Midnight Delta unit. I don't know a lot of the details myself, but he and his team are on a special assignment. I know it is critical, and they asked for you specifically."

Shit. Midnight Delta? "I won't let you down."

"I never thought you would, Preston."

Within fifteen minutes his phone was ringing. "Jack?"

"Lieutenant?"

"Call me Mason. Your captain told me you signed aboard. Great. We need you. You're to head to Dallas Memorial Hospital where Clint Archer will meet you."

"Captain Ivers was really vague on the details."

"Clint and other members of my team are working in conjunction with various arms of law enforcement to keep a family in protective custody. Our team rescued them from the Mexican jungle months ago, and since then they've been targeted, dammit," Mason swore. "We've pushed our way back in to help with their protection."

Mason was pissed, and Jack didn't blame him. "Okay, how can I help?"

"Part of my team is being deployed, I need to pull someone else to assist with this operation. I know you're the right man for the job."

Jack was stunned. Midnight Delta was legend. The team had been together for years, and after a mission had gone wrong, they didn't accept others onto their team. This was an honor.

"Definitely. I'll do whatever you need me to do."

"You're in San Antonio right now, correct?"

"Yes, Sir."

"I'm going to e-mail you all of the particulars including his contact information. Get in touch with him when you land. If you decide to drive because it's faster, contact him when you're close. I don't give a shit how you get there, just get there fast."

"Got it."

****

Jack looked at the delicate woman slumped over in the molded chair. She looked so alone, but then one of the senior men in the Midnight Delta SEAL unit sat down beside her and put his arm around her. He saw how she jerked away and found himself towering above the two before he even realized he crossed the room.

"Shit, I'm sorry, Beth," Clint said to the woman. "I forgot."

She didn't seem to hear him. Instead, she stared at Jack. He watched as her beautiful black eyes widened with fright. She took in a lungful of air and pushed deeper into the chair. He did what he always found helpful when his size intimidated children and animals, he crouched down, smiled, and slowly held out his hand.

"Hi, I'm Jack Preston." Out of the corner of his eye, he saw the other SEAL eyeing every move he made. But he gave most of his attention to the young woman in front of him. He watched as she considered whether to take his hand. When she finally touched her fingers to his, he could swear he felt a jolt of electricity. She took in a deep breath, and a flush suffused her face, and her eyes dilated.

"Elsbeth Hildago." Her accented voice flowed like warm honey through his system.

"Beth, remember, you need to say your name is Beth Ochoa from now on. Beth and her family are the reason you're here, Jack," Clint said, breaking the spell.

"Beth or Elsbeth?" Jack asked the woman in front of him.

"You may call me Beth," she whispered. Her Spanish accent made her voice sound like a melody.

Beth pulled her hand away and gripped it tightly with the other in her lap, but her gaze never wavered from his.

"How much have you been told?" Clint asked him.

"I know I'm now part of Midnight Delta." Jack still couldn't believe it.

"Our captain was looking for different places to hide members of her family. Places the corrupt members of the DEA, or any other agency, wouldn't find them. Your stepfather's ranch in San Antonio is damn near a fortress."

Jack settled back on his heels and gave Clint a knowing smile. He'd been courted for his family's wealth and property in the past, this was nothing new.

"Hell Archer, my family will be more than happy to make our ranch available for your operation. You

21

don't need to suddenly change your protocol and bring me onto the team. Whichever military personnel you bring will be welcome, it sure as hell doesn't need to be me." Jack shook his head in amusement and lifted his duffle to leave.

"Preston, if we didn't believe you were the SEAL for the job we would have done exactly that. We checked you out. Your record is exceptional. We want *and need* someone like you to join us."

Jack scrutinized Clint's face and saw nothing but honesty in the man's expression. He believed him.

"Beth, this is the man I told you about. I trust him implicitly. You'll be going with him. I wish you could stay with Lydia or your mother, but we know it will be safer if we split up your family. The rogue DEA agents aren't going to be looking for individuals. After what happened with the US Marshals, you'll be safe with Jack at his family's ranch."

Beth's face held a sense of desperation. It was clear she was scared and was looking to Clint for comfort. What kind of relationship did the two of them share? If it was intimate, why was she so scared of his touch?

"Only if you promise me Lydia will go with you. You're the only one who'll make her listen. She never takes care of herself."

"She'll go with me and I'll make her listen, even if I have to sit on her."

"Where will you go?"

"Some place safe. This should all be over by the time your father testifies."

"I won't see my family for that long?" Her bottom lip trembled, but then, she straightened her shoulders and looked at them. "Don't worry, I will do whatever is necessary. I won't be a burden to you. I promise."

"Of course you won't," Jack assured her. Clint caught his eye and gave him a nod.

"My bag is packed. When do we leave?"

"You can go in and say goodbye to your family. Please don't tell them you're going to San Antonio," Clint asked.

"I won't. You can trust me." Beth got up and left the room.

"How bad is the situation?" Jack asked Clint.

"It's bad. They've been in a safe house. Lydia was in the hospital recovering from her third bout of pneumonia, and somehow the Mexican drug cartel managed to turn one of the US Marshals, and he made an attempt on her life. "

"Why is the military involved?"

"We were originally involved because a congressman was implicated in the case with the cartel and the DEA. When their father testifies here in Texas, it will come out. The senator from Texas knows this, and he pulled some strings to get us to guard the family. Now the Marshals have fucked up, we're back in it."

"Damn." Because of his stepfather, Jack knew how complicated and nasty politics could get. He was impressed the senator had stepped in.

"We don't expect Beth to be targeted. So far, they've set their sights on Lydia, and as much as I hate it, we'll continue to use her to flush them out. What's most important for Beth is keeping her out of sight, and in an environment where she feels secure."

"Yeah, I noticed she's as skittish as a newborn foal."

"She and her family were kidnapped a few months ago by members of the cartel. Lydia almost died from the beating they gave her. Beth was subjected to abuse as well. She wasn't raped, but she was violated, and she's scared of men."

"My mom is at the ranch. She'll be a good person for Beth to talk to." Jack thought back to his younger years with his mother and birth father. Yeah, his mother would be the perfect person to help Beth.

Both men looked up as she walked back into the room.

"I'm ready." She'd been crying. But she bravely looked at the two of them, ready for whatever came next.

****

Jack Preston was so big. It was the first thing she noticed about him, but then he had crouched in front of her, and she started to see other things. His white-blonde hair, the laugh lines around his blue eyes, and he was younger than she originally thought.

But now they were in the big truck driving from Dallas to San Antonio, he seemed to take up all of the space in the truck. She'd been zoning, gazing at the scenery and thinking about Lydia. Somebody had tried to kill her sister while she was in the hospital. It was surreal.

"Beth, are you all right? You're awfully quiet."

She looked over at Jack Preston, and for the first time, she noticed she was alone in the truck with him. Suddenly, it was hard to breathe. It seemed like his big presence was taking up all of the oxygen. She gasped, trying to suck in air.

"Beth, are you okay?"

He was taking an exit off the freeway. She was having trouble even noticing the wildflowers along the highway. The world seemed to be turning into a long tunnel. Oh God, she was having a panic attack. She saw a diner from a long way off, it was a pinpoint in her narrow vision. Had the truck stopped?

She finally felt a breeze, and she started to hear a voice.

"Just breathe, Beth. Breathe the air. Can you smell the flowers? Just breathe, sweetheart. In and out. Breathe with me, in and out."

The breeze carried in the scent of the Texas wildflowers she had come to love. She felt a warm touch, so light, caressing up and down along the inside of her wrist in time with her breathing.

"In and out, Beth." Things began to come into focus. The windows were rolled down. They were in the parking lot of a diner. She looked over and saw Jack, his eyes held nothing but calm, none of the pity she'd gotten used to.

"There you are." He smiled. "Are you hungry? I sure am." Just like that, he made it seem like a panic attack was no big deal. She looked at his big hands holding her forearm, and he was still stroking her wrist. She looked up into his eyes, and he gave her a warm smile.

"You have the softest skin."

"You're touching me," she whispered, continuing to look into his eyes, and not feeling an immediate need to pull her arm out of his hands.

"Yes, I guess I am."

"Nobody touches me."

He cocked an eyebrow in question.

"Well, I never let any man touch me. How did you do that?" She looked back down to where his fingers still stroked her wrist. It felt good.

"Maybe a part of you knows you can trust me. At least this tiny little bit."

She looked back at him and got lost in his smile.

"That doesn't make any sense."

"Clint told you I was trustworthy and you trust him, right?"

"Oh, that must be it."

His stomach rumbled and he laughed. She gave a tentative smile. "Stay right there." He got out of his side of the truck, and before she could blink, he was at her side helping her out.

"I hope you like Texas barbecue because this is some of the best in the state." She wasn't sure she did, but she liked the fact she wasn't feeling uncomfortable with him anymore, so she was willing to try his barbecue.

27

Chapter Three

It seemed to take forever to get to the house after they went under the arch proclaiming Glendora Oaks Ranch.

"How big is this ranch anyway?" Beth asked Jack.

"It's been in my stepfather's family for generations. It's ten thousand acres."

"That must be a lot of responsibility." Jack gave her an approving look.

"It is good you understand. Most people see it as a pile of money. Richard, my dad, and his son, David, understand they are accountable to the people who depend on them. They're good men."

"Why aren't you working with them?"

"I had a different calling. I felt this need to serve and they understood. Richard always supported me. I've been very blessed with this new man my mother married." The way he said it made Beth wonder if perhaps the first man in Jack's life had not been a blessing.

Finally, they made their way around a gentle curve, and she gasped as she saw the beautiful ranch house in front of her.

"We're home."

A woman was waiting on the wraparound porch, her long white-blonde hair made it clear she was related to Jack. She leaned against one of the posts near the top step. Jack escorted Beth up the stairs.

"Mom, this is Beth Ochoa. This is my mom, Grace Preston."

"Hello, Mrs. Preston," she said as she held out her hand. Grace carefully stepped forward and wrapped Beth in a warm hug.

"Welcome to our ranch, Beth. I am sure we are going to be good friends, and please call me Grace."

"Mom, where's your cane?"

"It's right by the door, you worry-wart. I knew I was going to have your strong arm to lean on for the rest of the day, so I left it there." She gave her son a breathtaking smile.

She turned to Beth. "I'm lucky to have three men who I can lean on, so I rarely need to use my cane. Come into the house with me. Jack will take your things to your room. It's been a long drive, and you might want to nap. Whenever you're ready, Rosa will start dinner."

"I don't want you to wait dinner for my sake."

"It's not a problem. If we're hungry, we'll snack," Jack assured her. "Go and take your time, Beth. Mom and I always find something to talk about." He winked at his mom and she chuckled.

****

A few hours later, Beth met Grace's husband, Richard, and his son, David. Where Jack was light, these men were good looking with dark skin and hair, and they made her nervous. Jack had noticed it. He arranged for her to sit next to him at dinner.

"Jack told us you're here undercover," David said.

"I guess I am. It sounds more romantic than it really is. I'm not allowed to discuss it really." David tilted his head and gave her a crooked smile.

"Okay, what can you tell us? Before all this happened were you in school? You don't look old enough to be a career girl and if you were married, I'm sure your husband wouldn't let you out of his sight."

Beth always felt uncomfortable answering questions about herself, even before the mess with her father. She tried to give as few details as possible.

"I help out with my father's business here and there, and I spend time at the recreation center with my special kids."

"Special kids?" Grace asked.

"Just some kids that need a little extra tutoring."

"What a wonderful way to give back. How many children do you work with?"

"Just a few," Beth answered slowly.

"Do you teach them to read?"

"I help them with whatever they need." Beth looked down at her plate and toyed with her food.

"Well, that's wonderful. Not a lot of people give back these days."

"It's really not a big deal. I have a sister who is three years older, and she is getting her masters in computer science. She double-majored in computer science and in criminology. Now she is the interesting one."

"It seems to me like you're both pretty fascinating." Grace smiled warmly.

"Have you ever been on a working ranch?" David asked. "I can show you around tomorrow."

Beth concentrated on the Spanish rice she was eating, and tried to think of a way out of the invitation.

"David, give the girl a little bit of time to acclimate," Grace chided. Beth was able to swallow.

"Just remember, when you need a tour, I'm your man. Jack probably doesn't remember the difference between a horse and a cow." Beth looked up, surprised this man would be putting down his brother. But when she saw his face, she realized he had been teasing.

"Watch it, cowboy. I can still ride circles around you."

"Bullshit. You've gotten soft." That was followed by laughter even Beth had to join in on. The idea of Jack having gone soft was ridiculous. She liked how the family interacted.

"Jack, tell me more about the rescue efforts in Las Flores," Richard requested.

"The devastation left by the earthquake was horrific, Dad. But it was great seeing how many relief agencies came in the first week. Then I was stunned to see how quickly it started to dwindle."

"It was all over the news the first week, and then we didn't hear anything," David concurred.

"You were in Las Flores?" Beth asked.

"He was there right after the earthquake happened," Grace answered.

"I didn't think SEALs did rescue efforts like that."

"We don't normally, but there was a hostage situation we got involved in. After it was resolved, we stayed to help."

"Then he got his father involved in coordinating donations for the people. Richard is involved in charities so he might be able to help."

David snorted. "Don't let Mom fool you. Dad's on the board of directors of one of the largest charities in Texas. He can get donations out of a stone."

"Was the hostage thing dangerous?"

"Everything Jack does is dangerous," David said with a twinkle in his eye.

"That's nothing to tease about. Whenever Jack is deployed and I turn on the news I'm worried to death," Grace said. Richard reached over and put his arm around the back of her chair.

"You know our son is the best at what he does," Richard said in a soothing tone. "He can take care of himself."

"It still doesn't stop a mother from worrying."

Beth looked through her lashes at Jack. She could easily see him as one of the men who rescued her and her family in the Mexican jungle. He had the same air about him. She felt safe with him, but she knew if the wrong people came around they'd be in trouble. She was amazed she was comfortable with Jack. It was certainly an anomaly. Her reaction to Richard and David was more normal. They made her nervous.

The conversation changed to the running of the ranch while Beth enjoyed the meal Rosa had prepared. Grace guided a great deal of the conversation. It was clear the three men at the table adored her. At one point, David said something to make Richard give a sudden laugh and Beth dropped her glass of wine. Nobody made a big deal of it. Jack blotted the liquid, and slowly covered her trembling hand with his. Like in the truck, the small touch helped soothe her.

As the conversation resumed, he let go of her hand and leaned over to her and whispered, "It will get easier, I promise."

God, she hoped so.

Later that night, Beth took a better look around the room they had given her to stay in. It was lovely, like something out of a movie. Beth took advantage of the little vanity with the padded bench and the three-way mirror to brush her hair. It was the first time in forever she was able to look at herself in the mirror without flinching.

Even before the time in the jungle, she had been afraid of men. She shied away from the whys and wherefores. No point. But something amazing was going on in front of the mirror tonight. Normally she thought her looks were dirty and shameful somehow, but not as much tonight. Today, for a few minutes with Jack, she was a little more like the girl she'd once been. It felt good. Wouldn't it be nice if she could take back just a little bit of what had been stolen?

****

By the third day, Beth really began to feel comfortable in her new surroundings. The night before at dinner, Jack asked Beth if she knew how to ride a horse. When she said she didn't, he asked if she would like to learn. Everyone seemed to be staring at her, but it was Grace's encouraging smile that made her say 'yes.'

Now she was on the porch waiting for Jack to take her to the stables. He opened the door loudly behind her, and she turned. She knew he did it on purpose. Jack had an uncanny way of entering a room silently and scaring her, but after seeing her fright, he'd begun to make noise announcing his presence.

"You ready?"

"I think so." Beth paused, and really thought about it. Then said with more confidence. "Yes, I'm ready."

They walked down to the corral. Jack shortened his steps and she was able to keep up. When they reached the stable, two horses were saddled and waiting for them.

"Is this the horse I get to ride?" She looked at the beautiful red horse and immediately fell in love. She looked at Jack for confirmation. Jack smiled and nodded.

"You're such a pretty girl," Beth crooned, as she petted her neck.

"Boy."

"What?"

"He's a pretty boy." She looked from Jack to the horse.

"You're such a handsome boy. Look at you, with your beautiful hair, and your warm eyes. Aren't you a flirt?" And he was. He was already leaning into her hands obviously enjoying the attention.

"I should have thought of this, but I didn't. You're going to need some help getting onto Bay. He obviously loves you, he's really well-mannered, and won't move as you mount him, but I will need to touch you. Is that alright?"

Beth looked from Jack to the horse and bit her lip. Jack was worried and she hated it. Hated she needed to be treated like spun glass.

"If you tell me what you're going to do I should be fine." She tried, but she couldn't stop the tremor in her voice.

"Sweetheart, your courage amazes me."

"Well, it shouldn't. I should be passed this."

"Ah Beth, you need to be kind to yourself. This takes time and patience, and I think all things considered you're doing amazingly well. Now put your foot in the stirrup. I'm going to put my hands on your waist and help you into the saddle, okay?"

Beth held her breath and nodded. She did what he instructed, and he gave her an encouraging smile before settling his hands around her waist, plucking her off the ground, and putting her on top of the horse.

"*Dios.*" The man was strong.

"Are you okay?"

She was having trouble catching her breath.

"Beth, are you okay? Do you need to get down?" His hand hovered over her leg as he looked at her.

"I'm all right," she whispered. He waited. "Really. I'm fine."

He gave her one last look and winked.

"Okay, here are the reins. I'm going to help put your other foot in the stirrup." He did as he said with an economy of motion. Soon, he took back the reins and was on the other horse and leading her around the corral.

She was riding a horse! She had handled his touch!

He looked back at her.

"That's an awfully big grin, Miss Beth. Care to share with the class?"

"I'm having a great time." She leaned over and patted Bay. He nickered.

"I think your horse likes you." Jack kept them going at a slow and consistent pace around the corral.

"Shouldn't we drive faster?" He laughed.

"I think we're *driving* fast enough, sweetheart." Jack easily rode his horse, as well as held the lead for Bay so he could guide him around the paddock. She admired how the man looked in the saddle. She might be nervous around men, but it didn't stop her from noticing handsome works of art. Jack's butt in a saddle was definitely a work of art.

Bay made an odd step and she gripped the saddle horn and squeaked. Jack's head whipped around.

"Are you okay?"

"I'm fine." But he must have heard the tremble in her voice.

"I think that's enough for one day."

For an instant, she considered protesting, kind of like as a child when her parents wanted her to come in from riding her bicycle. But she subdued the thought and nodded. They made their way back to the stables, and she didn't have a panic attack when he helped her off the horse.

She helped Jack brush Bay and fed him some carrots. When she got back to the ranch house, she realized she'd actually ridden a horse. It was like she was floating on air.

****

"*Chica*, what are you doing in here?"

"I was wondering if I could come and help cook dinner."

"Help or cook?" Rosa asked. Beth blushed.

"That's what I thought. You like to cook, don't you?"

"I love to cook, bake, and clean. I'm weird," Beth admitted.

Rosa laughed.

"No, you're not weird. Most women these days wouldn't admit they like caring for a home. I like doing those things. So does Grace. She'd do more if it weren't for her hip." Rosa bustled over to the refrigerator and opened it. "I have pork, chicken, and beef of course. What would you like to make for tonight's meal?"

"What kind of apples do you have?"

"Come and look." Rosa invited.

Beth peered into the crisper and was delighted to find some Fuji apples.

"Herbed pork and apples and apple crisp for dessert."

"Let's get to it."

Beth rubbed her hands together. This was going to be fun. They had the pork roast in the oven when Grace came in the kitchen.

"I see you ladies have been busy. I was coming to get some sweet tea, but I think this calls for a glass of wine." Beth giggled at the thought of the three of them having wine in the afternoon.

"I'll pour. Chablis?" Rosa asked.

"Is that what you want to drink?" Grace asked.

"Yep."

"Well okay then. How about you, Beth?" It all seemed so naughty and she loved it. She measured out the brown sugar and said Chablis sounded wonderful.

"You know we'll have to taste test this before the men can have any for dessert," Grace warned her.

"As a matter of fact, we might have to do a lot of taste testing. You should probably double the batch, *Chica*." Beth giggled as she took a sip of her wine.

"So even though you're undercover, what can you tell us about yourself?" Grace asked.

"I'm not sure." Beth continued measuring out ingredients.

"Can you tell us how old you are?"

"I'm almost twenty-three."

"You have a sister, right?" Rosa asked as she pulled out more apples for Grace to cut up.

"Yes, Lydia. She's brilliant. She's working on her masters in computer science. She wants to work in criminal justice."

"In Mexico? *Madre de Dios.* They'll eat her alive!" Rosa exclaimed.

"It scares me to death. But there are animals who need to be brought to justice." Beth stirred the mixture so hard some flew out of the bowl. She looked up and found both women looking at her oddly.

"Are you okay, Beth?" Grace asked.

"Oh," she looked down at the mess, embarrassed. "I'm so sorry."

"It's not a problem." Rosa used a paper towel and scooped up the splatter. "There, all fixed."

"Beth, I agree, there are some bad people. Is there anything you want to talk about?" She looked at the kind faces of the two women and gave a small smile.

"I'm fine."

"Well, if you ever do want to talk we'll be here for you. In the meantime, I think you need a refill," Grace said.

Beth giggled. The two women looked at one another.

"That's a nice sound, Beth," Grace said.

"What sounds nice?"

"You giggling. You don't do it enough."

"My sister Lydia said the same thing to me. She said I'd gotten too serious."

"You should listen to her, she's older," Rosa said knowingly. Beth snorted.

"My sister might be book smart, but for the last year she's needed a keeper. She doesn't take care of herself and it's my job to make sure she does."

"I wish I had a sister," Grace said quietly. "Lydia sounds lucky to have you."

"Not that she thinks so. Most of the time she thinks she needs to protect me. But trust me, it's been the other way around. She's had pneumonia three times in the last six months. She would have let herself die instead of asking for help."

"No, really?" Rosa gasped.

"Yes! The only reason I agreed to leave her side is because the man who is with her is in love with her and he'll make sure she's taken care of. Of course, she'll fight him every inch of the way." Beth giggled. Both women grinned, and Grace poured more wine.

"What do you do besides run roughshod over your sister?"

"The school I tutor at is connected to an orphanage. A lot of the kids have been abandoned by their parents because they were mentally disabled. I work with some of them." Beth took the cut apples from

Grace and spread them over the mixture at the bottom of the pan.

Grace nodded to Rosa, who refilled Beth's glass.

"How do you work with them?"

Beth took another couple of sips of her wine as she put the dessert into the oven. "I spend almost forty hours a week as a teacher's aide. I've learned a lot from the international volunteers who have come in to help. Besides being a wife and mother, I always wanted to be a teacher for the learning impaired."

Beth hiccupped, and they all laughed.

"I'm curious. Why haven't you gone to school?"

"I didn't want to be alone on a campus," Beth said in a sad voice. "Can we not talk about me anymore?" Rosa and Grace looked at one another.

"Have I told you about my boyfriend Chuck?" Rosa asked in a bright tone.

By the time the first dessert was ready to test, they each had three glasses of wine. Beth got to hear about Rosa's on-again, off again boyfriend, Chuck. They giggled at the numerous ways he managed to work his way back into Rosa's good graces. Beth hadn't had such a good time in forever.

"Ladies, are you holding out on us?" Richard and Jack filled the doorway of the kitchen, and they had matching smiles on their faces.

"It's Beth's fault," Grace quickly said.

Beth felt the blood rushing to her cheeks and shot the woman a mortified glance.

"Easy Beth, she's just teasing you," Jack said as he sauntered into the kitchen.

"What smells so damn good, and what has you all giggling so hard?" Richard asked as he grabbed a spoon out of the silverware drawer. Jack followed suit, and both men took large scoops of the dessert.

"I think they figured out what smells so good, don't you Rosa?" Grace asked.

"And what else could have us laughing this hard? It's *mi amor*, Chuck."

"That'd do it," Jack said as he shifted to stand next to Beth, his hip touching hers.

"Rosa, you've outdone yourself with this apple crisp, and if the roast tastes as good as it smells, dinner will be outstanding," Richard said as he went to stand next to his wife.

"That's all Beth's doing. She offered to cook tonight."

"Is that right?" Jack said as he looked at her. "Aren't you just full of surprises?"

"I think she is, Jack. I think she is," Richard said. Rosa and Grace thought it was hysterical, and Beth laughed as well.

"I'm going to lock up the wine until dinner," Jack went to get the bottle and found it empty. "Well, I guess I'm too late." That just made the three of them laugh harder.

"I think dinner might be late tonight, Dad."

Chapter Four

The day in the kitchen was a bit of a breakthrough for Beth. She continued to help Rosa, and his mother joined in where she was able. The three of them became thick as thieves. Beth also totally took over the kitchen garden responsibilities from Rosa. It was clear Beth was in her element around the house and the ladies, but the men still made her somewhat nervous—David and Richard especially.

She didn't tremble every time Richard or David came into the room. Of course, both men were aware of the fact that they made her uncomfortable and were careful to always have Grace or Rosa with them.

Jack worked every day to ensure that she was more and more at ease with his touch. He did little things like brushing up against her or making sure they sat close enough on the couch their legs touched. It's the same kind of gentling technique Richard had taught him years ago with horses.

Jack was looking around the big house for Beth when he finally found her in the library folding up a thick wad of paper and putting it into an envelope. He smiled. In his mind's eye, he could picture the children who received these letters and he was positive that they made the kid's days brighter.

"Here's my latest bunch of letters to be mailed out."

Jack looked at the envelopes with the block letters on them.

"There's not as many as last time, why not?"

Beth's eyes went wide. "You noticed?"

"Where's Carmen's letter?"

"In the last letter that came through via the courier, they said Carmen had been moved to another school with no forwarding address."

"Does that happen a lot?"

"No, not very often at all. I'm hoping, in this case, her parents might have taken her back to live with them."

"I don't understand, isn't this like a school? Don't they live with their parents?"

"All of the children I work with live in the orphanage. In most cases, their parents aren't dead they left their children there because they couldn't take care of them on their own."

"Ah damn, and you were worried they would think you were one more person who had abandoned them."

"That's it! It's so important for them to have continuity. No matter what, I write a letter every week."

"How come when I've asked you about this, you haven't wanted to tell me about it?"

"It's just a little volunteer thing I do during the week."

"That's not the way Mom tells it."

"Oh, your mom told you about what I do?" Beth looked uncomfortable.

"Well, I've asked you a couple of times and you've brushed it off. When mom explained it to me, I realized what an undertaking it is." Jack thumbed through the six thick envelopes.

"I guess." She watched his hands.

"Mom said you're not a teacher."

"I'm more of a teacher's aide. I don't have the credentials to be a teacher."

"But you wanted to be. You said so." She looked at the floor, and then finally back at him.

"You've seen me, I'm not good around people. Being on campus makes me uncomfortable. I was thinking about taking some on-line courses." Her voice trailed off. She looked so sad. He tried to think of something to put a smile back on her face.

"Tell me about your favorite student."

"Viola. Definitely, Viola. She still can't speak much, but when I first met her she didn't have any language at all. Everybody had given up on her, they didn't think she was capable of communicating. But you could see it in her eyes that she understood things and she was frustrated we couldn't understand her grunts and gestures. Now she has about one hundred words." Beth was grinning from ear to ear.

"Can she read the letter you sent to her?"

"I drew some pictures and someone will read the rest to her." Viola's letter had definitely been the thickest.

Jack wondered if he could figure out a way for Beth to take some on-line classes while she was here at the ranch.

Jack's phone buzzed. "I'll make sure these get out."

"Thanks, Jack."

****

"You're looking stressed." Jack stared at her.

"Not stressed," Beth said as she hung up the phone. "Worried? A little angry? Concerned?" She walked around the library and touched the bronze horse on the bookshelf. Then turned, and stroked her hand against the leather of the chair.

"Concerned. Maybe worried?" She struggled to find the right word as she finally stopped next to the desk where she had hung up the phone. She looked at Jack, who had a bemused expression on his face.

"What?" she asked crossly.

"I think the word you're looking for is stressed."

"Fine, I'm stressed," she snapped.

"Want to talk about it?"

"No." Beth walked around the library again. She touched the horse, and then stroked the chair, and was finally in front of Jack one more time.

"I need to get out of the house," she told him.

"Your wish is my command."

Did he have to be so agreeable all of the time?

Instead of going through the great room and out the front door, he took her out the mudroom in the back of the house, and they ended up near the kitchen garden. Boone came trotting up, and she bent down to give the hound a thorough petting. Beth breathed a sigh of relief. She loved it there. He opened the little gate and they went inside.

"I don't think I've ever seen the plants take off when Rosa was in charge of this garden."

Beth swung around and looked up at him.

"For God's sake, never say that to her." She knew it was true. The garden had been in desperate need of care and attention when she had first taken over. Now the plants were thriving. But the last thing she needed was for someone to make comparisons between her abilities and Rosa's.

"Beth, Rosa would be the first person to say you're doing a better job than she was."

"Jack, you just don't understand. Never say anything, okay?" She watched him finally nod in agreement, and she sighed in relief. For God's sake, men could be so dense. The last thing she wanted was to have Rosa's feelings hurt.

"Do you want to tell me what had you so upset in the library?"

"I thought we agreed I was stressed."

"Okay, stressed. What has you so stressed?"

"Nothing new." Beth blew the bangs out of her eyes. "My sister."

Jack looked perplexed. "I thought she was your big sister. From everything you've told me she always protects you. Why would you be stressed about her?"

"Yes, Lydia would take a bullet for me. Hell, she'd shove me out of the way, and wave 'take me, take me'. But at the same time she doesn't have the sense God gave a gnat when it comes to taking care of herself."

Beth saw the confusion on Jack's face.

"Look, I know I talk about her being all computer science, and 'I want to be a cop' one day girl. But this is the same woman who needs to be told to go to the hospital or you will die. This is the same girl who will forget to eat because she's studying too much. This is the same girl who will put herself in danger and damn the consequences. She needs a keeper, and it's been me. I was hoping it would be Clint, but now I'm not so sure."

Jack still looked confused, and *now* she was getting angry at *him*. The man needed to keep up. "So what happened on your call to make you stressed?"

"She won't tell me what's going on! She's lying to me. I can tell. I can always tell when she'd glossing over the truth to make me feel better about something so I don't worry. Doesn't she understand it makes me worry more?"

"Beth." Jack started carefully. "Your sister sounds like a really capable lady. What's more, she's with one of the deadliest men on the planet. I don't think you need to worry."

"Haven't you listened to a word I said?! Lydia will put herself in danger and not think twice about it. She needs to be held back."

"Clint is there to do it."

"I don't know about that, Jack. It seems to me that he's a danger junkie. Are you sure he'd be cautious? She needs to be sat on. What happens if he doesn't understand she takes stupid risks?"

"Oh sweetheart, didn't you tell me before Clint cares about Lydia. Really cares about her?"

"Yes," she admitted slowly.

"Then he knows her," Jack assured her. "He's not going to let her come to any harm, nor is he going to let her take unnecessary risks. One of the ways we survive is to be smart about our risks, Beth. And he sure as shit won't let Lydia take them."

"Really?" she asked.

"Really."

Beth saw the sincerity in Jack's blue eyes and blew out a sigh of relief. "Because something is going on. Can you try to find out from Clint why she's being evasive? I'm not imagining things."

"I'll call him. Chances are you're not imagining things. But I am sure he will make sure your sister is taken care of."

"Thank you, it would make me feel less stressed."

He smiled at her. "Anything to have you feeling less angry, worried, and concerned," he teased.

****

His dad called him out on it the fourth week she was on the ranch.

"What are your intentions with Beth? You do realize what she's gone through, don't you?"

Jack was on his computer in his father's study. He was checking his e-mail, knowing something was up, because the calls between Lydia and Beth were becoming more infrequent. Taking note of the closed door, he realized his dad intended to have one of *those* kinds of talks. They didn't happen often, but when they did they were serious.

"I don't have any official intentions regarding Beth."

"Funny, because it sure looks like you're pursuing her pretty hard."

"What are you talking about? I haven't even kissed her." Jack looked across the desk at his dad in surprise.

55

"I expected better of you Jack, I really did."

"Wait a minute. I like her. A lot. I think she is beautiful, smart, and has a big heart. She needs her confidence bolstered is all."

Richard stared at him, his eyes sad and condemning. Jack didn't like seeing that look in his father's eyes. He closed his laptop and really thought about Beth Hidalgo, which was easy to do since she was on his mind morning, noon, and night. Even at this moment, he could take a deep breath and he swore he smelled her sweet, fragrant scent. She was dazzling. Not in any sort of diamond bright way. No, she was like the opal his mother wore, creamy and silky with so many colors swirling beneath the surface.

"You didn't hear a word I said, did you?"

"Huh?"

"What's Beth's middle name?"

"Sarah," Jack answered.

"What's her favorite movie?"

"Lord of the Rings."

"Is she right or left handed?"

"Left."

"What's her favorite color?"

"Rust. She says it's like seeing the brown of the earth mixed with a ruby."

Richard got up and walked towards the door. "Where are you going?"

"I was wrong."

"About what?"

"You might not have any official intentions with her, but your heart is definitely in the right place."

Jack watched as the door closed behind his dad. His e-mail pinged. Clint wanted him to call. It worried him because there was a scheduled call between Lydia and Beth tonight.

The men had arranged for phones for the women and their parents to use that couldn't be traced. Beth talked to her parents regularly, but her talks with Lydia had gotten more and more sporadic.

"What's up?"

"Jack, we have a situation. This might be the last call for a while," Clint's voice was tense.

Jack asked the only question that mattered. "Is Beth in danger?"

Clint chuckled. "I knew I liked you."

"Answer the fucking question."

"No, they've targeted Lydia again. She and I are going on the run. I'm sure glad Mason decided to bring you in on this. You're who I would have chosen too."

"Why?"

"It was the operation in Kuwait."

Jack rubbed the back of his neck. He hated thinking about that mission. Not so much how it had played out. They'd rescued the hostage, and the plan was perfectly executed. It was the shape the young teenager was in by the time they'd gotten to him. Jack had kept tabs on Kevin, and he was having problems to this day.

"So what do you mean by 'targeted' Lydia? What happened?"

"There was another attempt on Lydia's life. They're all in. We're going off the grid. There will be no more calls after this one. I know it's going to be hard on both of the sisters, but they're tough. They'll deal with it.

"If Lydia is anything like Beth, then yes she is."

"Lydia's amazing." The admiration in Clint's voice was clear.

"So is Beth. Look, Clint, I need to say this. Beth is worried Lydia will take unnecessary risks."

"What do you mean?"

"She says Lydia doesn't take care of herself. That she needs a keeper."

"Well I'm the fucking keeper, now aren't I?" Clint growled. "You tell Beth I've got her covered."

"I already did."

"Good. Now let's get the two of them on the phone together."

****

Beth watched the door close behind Jack as she waited for Lydia to get on the line.

"Beth?"

"Lydia. What's going on? Jack said this is the last call we're going to have for a while. What's wrong?"

"Nothing big." She sounded strained.

"You're lying. You sound exactly the same way every time I ask if you're feeling sick, and you say you're fine. Only then you're coughing up a lung. Tell me the truth." Beth heard the pain in her voice, and tried to tamp it down but she couldn't. She was sick of people treating her like she needed to be protected. She was an adult dammit.

"Look, it wasn't a big deal." Lydia paused.

"Now I *know* it was a big deal. Every time you started a conversation with our parents saying something wasn't a big deal, it was a *huge* deal. Tell me. C'mon it's me you're talking to."

"Somebody tried to kill us. They came into our bedroom. Clint saved us. Oh my God, it was like something out of a movie." Beth heard both the terror and admiration in her sister's voice. "I thought we were going to die. But he saved us," she ended in a watery whisper.

"Oh Lydia, I hate this. But I'm thanking God he was there for you." She waited while Lydia calmed herself.

"Hey wait a minute, did you say, *our* bedroom?" She was met by dead silence, and then Lydia giggled, sounding almost like the girl Beth remembered.

"Oh my God, I caught you, didn't I? You're totally doing it with Clint! Lydia and Clint, sitting in a tree, doing far more than kiss...I...N... G." They both laughed uproariously.

"Beth, I think I love him. I really think I'm in love." A huge weight rolled off Beth's heart. For so long she'd worried about her sister. Lydia was constantly doing for everyone else. Taking on other people's burdens and putting herself last. The idea she would be grabbing the brass ring with such a great guy made Beth ecstatic.

"Say something."

"I can't, my smile is too big. It's hard to form words around it."

"Oh, yeah, I hate it when I can't form words around it." It took Beth a second to figure out what her sister meant, and then she started to blush.

"You're blushing aren't you?" Lydia laughed.

"You don't know me," Beth protested.

Lydia sighed. "I can't wait until this whole thing is over and we can be together again. I want you to have the life you deserve. I know you want to have a family. I know the shit in the jungle was bad, but you were working through it in counseling with Nancy. I want you back in counseling so you can have a man, a houseful of kids, and a dirty house to clean."

Beth couldn't see past the tears in her eyes. "That sounds perfect."

"For you, I know it does."

"It's never going to happen for me. We both have to be realistic."

"You have to have faith. Come on, you never missed Sunday school. You have lots more faith than I do." Beth smiled wanly.

"Tell me about Clint."

"I can't, honey. He's telling me our time is up." Beth clutched the phone. She didn't want to hang up.

"Stay safe Lydia, you're my favorite sister."

"You're my favorite sister too. I love you baby girl."

Clint must have called Jack on his phone because he came in soon after and found her crying.

"Do you want to talk about it?"

"How tough are you SEALs?"

"Sweetheart, we're the toughest things out there."

"Good. I don't want my sister to die."

"She won't. Clint is going to keep her safe."

"You're right. He carried her through the jungle, did I tell you?" He nodded, and she remembered she'd told him before.

"I need to get to bed."

"Are you sure you don't want to talk?"

"Not tonight."

"Let me walk you to your room." Beth let out an unsteady laugh.

"Want to tell me what the laugh is for?"

"You know you're kind of rich."

"Why do you say that?"

"I've never needed someone to walk me to my room in their own house. Your house is pretty big, Jack."

"Dad's wealthy not me." She stared at him with a knowing smirk.

"Okay, I might be a little bit wealthy, but don't tell the other SEALs, they might make fun of me on the playground." She giggled like she knew he wanted.

When they got in front of her bedroom door, he opened it.

"Can I give you a hug?" She thought about it and realized she wanted a hug from him.

"Please."

Jack folded her into his arms as gently as he hugged his mother. But she didn't have any family feelings towards Jack. No, he felt like a man, and it felt good to be in his arms. Not just because he was her protector, but because he was Jack Preston, and he was fast becoming her new faith.

Chapter Five

Jack didn't think anything of it when his parents decided to take a long weekend in Dallas. It was something they did at least once a month, and easy enough with the family helicopter. Then David left on a trip to purchase livestock for the ranch, and Rosa visited her sister down in Houston.

He and Beth were in the great room, both reading books when the rain started. "Thank God everyone left as early as they did. This is going to be a hell of a rainstorm."

"Wh-What?"

"Yep, we're going to get thunder, lightning, and hail. The hands have battened down the hatches."

"What does that mean?"

Jack paused. "I love your accent, but I never really think about English not being your first language. You understand and speak it so well. Hell, you're even reading a book in English. Batten down the hatches is an old sailing term, meaning tie everything down so it doesn't fall overboard. The guys made sure everything is safe and the livestock is inside."

"How long will the storm last?"

"Until tomorrow." She bit her lip, and the book in her hand trembled. "Are you scared of storms?"

"A little."

"We can leave some lights on tonight."

She gave a grateful smile. They continued to read until she started yawning. He watched as her head drooped, and finally he convinced her it was time for bed. The light turned on underneath her bedroom door, and then he turned on the hallway light in case she got up in the middle of the night.

A loud crack of thunder woke him up. He was out of bed and in a crouch before he knew what happened. He gave a rueful grin. At least, he knew his training was still alive and kicking. Pulling on a pair of sweatpants, he made his way to the kitchen and got some juice. He was halfway up the stairs back to his room when the lights went out and he heard a scream.

Like a shot, he was at Beth's door and in her room. He scanned it and saw nothing more than her slight body tangled in the comforter, thrashing. "Beth?"

She was pleading in Spanish, begging for help. Begging to be released. Begging for mercy.

It hit him like a punch in the gut. He knelt down beside the bed. "Beth? Can you hear me?" he whispered in Spanish. He didn't want to talk too loudly and scare her. Touching her didn't seem like the best idea either.

"Beth." She was rolling around on the bed and came close to the side when she began to slip off he caught her. She screamed and woke up, and he immediately placed her back onto the middle of the bed.

"Beth, you had a nightmare. The power went out. You're safe. It's me, Jack."

She scrambled backward, whimpering. He continued to repeat that she'd had a nightmare and she was safe. After the longest minutes of his life, she quieted. God, it made him want to kill somebody.

"Jack?"

"Yes, sweetheart, it's me."

"Turn on the lights. Please turn on the lights."

"Oh, baby, if I could I would, but the power went out."

She whimpered, and slowly reached out. Realizing she probably couldn't see as well as he could in the dark, he said, "I'm going to hold your hand, okay?"

"Oh yes." He gently grasped her hand and she gripped it hard.

"Let me get a flashlight or some candles." He brought her hand to his lips and kissed her knuckles. He felt her slowly let go, and then got up and headed for the door.

"Don't leave!" He turned around and she was kneeling on the bed, reaching out to him.

"Do you want to go with me?"

"Yes!" She crawled across the bed and almost fell off the end. He caught her and she froze.

"Shhh, it's okay." He eased her down so her feet met the floor. She clutched his arms and didn't let go.

"Sweetheart, you're going to have release me so we can get the candles." He brushed down her arms and touched her hands to get her to let go. Another crack of thunder, and then a flash of lightning lit up the room. She screamed and slammed backward. The bed hit behind her knees and she fell flat on her back onto the mattress.

"NOOOOO!" she shrieked.

"Beth." He tried to get her attention.

She screamed in Spanish. The storm had catapulted her back in time to the horror of the jungle. He couldn't say anything to bring her out of it. She was fighting ghosts. Once again, she was close to falling off the side of the bed, and once again he caught her before she fell.

"Don't touch me. Please. Mercy." Her voice trailed off, and she went limp.

The faint gray light from the window allowed him to see her face as she lay there staring up at him, with tears leaking into the hair at her temples. He took the opportunity to try to get through to her. He crooned and whispered, praying she would hear him and feel safe.

She began to shake and then shudder. "J-Jack?"

"Yes, it's me, baby."

"I'm so scared." He ached to hold her. Her trembling was tearing him apart.

"Tell me what I can do. I'll do whatever you need."

The sound of the rain was punctuated by her heavy breathing. He carefully pulled the comforter around her and she clutched it tight.

"Don't leave me."

Jack sat on the bed, held out his arm so it gleamed in a shaft of moonlight, and waited. He hoped she would take the small bit of comfort he was offering. Slowly, she leaned into him, and finally, she was snuggled into his side.

She moaned when another boom of thunder sounded. He put a gentle arm around her and pulled her close, she dropped the stranglehold she had on the comforter and instead gripped his forearm. Jack froze. Had he miscalculated? She pulled his arm against her, holding him closer to her quaking body.

"I've got you, Beth. I won't let anyone hurt you, I promise."

Lightning lit the sky. She started to cry.

He couldn't stand it, in one swift movement, he scooped her up and she was on his lap.

****

Beth woke up feeling disoriented. She had a headache. She wasn't lying down. She was sitting up, well, reclining—sort of. She jerked awake, and her head hit Jack's chin. He gave a muffled grunt.

"I had a nightmare, didn't I?"

"It was the storm."

She looked around the room, the lights weren't on, but a little bit of moonlight was coming through the windows, and then she heard the harsh rain outside.

"I hate the rain. We had to walk through the jungle in the rain for five days." She peered up at him through her eyelashes. He was waiting for her to continue. God, she needed to just talk about it. This she could, at least, talk about.

"Before the rain, before the rescue, it was... it was..."

"Take your time." His calm voice and kind eyes allowed her to continue.

"Mama and Papa were tied up in the shack. They pulled me and Lydia out. There were four of them."

"Two started with Lydia and two started with me. To begin with I did what they said." She looked away from Jack, not wanting to see the condemnation in his eyes. He cupped her chin and lifted it.

"It's okay, sweetheart, you did what you needed to survive."

"I-I, I took off my clothes like they told me to. But then, they started to touch me and I went crazy. I fought so hard, I screamed, and kicked, and bit them, and they laughed. They hurt me, and bruised me, but I wasn't raped." She started as Jack brushed his lips against her temple.

"Thank God."

"They were about to when Lydia yelled she was going to be more fun because she was willing." Beth stopped talking as she relived the terrifying time in the jungles of Mexico.

Beth realized she was crying because Jack was rocking her and murmuring into her hair. She dragged herself back to the present and continued her story. "They left me naked in the dirt, and I was crying and scrambling for my clothes. The next thing I knew one of the men was screaming. I looked over and he was on the ground writhing in pain and Lydia was being dragged into the cabin by her hair."

"They whipped her. I thought she was going to die. *Dios*." She buried her face in his chest and sobbed. "She almost did die. She still gets sick because of what they did to her, and it's all my fault. She was trying to protect me."

"It wasn't your fault, sweetheart. You are her baby sister, she loves you and, of course, she wanted to save you."

"She suffers because of me."

Jack shifted, pulling her even closer, so her face was now nestled in the crook of his neck. He kissed the top of her head.

"One day, you might have a daughter and understand she did what came naturally."

"But I can't. I could never allow that kind of touch. I will never marry. I will never have children." More tears dripped from her eyes.

"Ah, Beth."

"All I wanted was to be a wife, a mother, and a teacher. They took that from me. I will never be able to stand having a man touch me like that."

"Maybe with time." Jack's hold was gentle, and his voice soothing.

She heard the hope. It matched what she felt in her own heart. But she knew better. Too much had gone on in her life. She was broken.

"No, Jack. Not even with all the time in the world." He needed to know this. She refused to let this wonderful man live with a dream that could never come true.

The lights came on. They looked at one another, and for the first time, she saw something besides encouragement in Jack's eyes. She saw sorrow.

Chapter Six

Jack had enough. It had been one week since the thunderstorm, and Beth had barely been out of her room. Rosa used guilt to get her back to the garden, but nothing Jack said persuaded her to come horseback riding. Finally, Jack sent in his secret weapon.

"Well?"

"She's coming on the picnic." His mother smiled at him.

"You're a miracle worker."

"I think it was the temptation of the Texas bluebonnets. Telling her they weren't going to be in season much longer was what did it."

"I'll see you and Dad out front. I have the horses ready, and Rosa packed a great lunch."

"Pretty sure of yourself, aren't you?" His mother grinned.

"Nope, pretty sure about you." He gave his mom a gentle squeeze.

He'd considered everything Beth said and didn't say, the night of the thunderstorm. The woman might have said there was no hope, but in his line of work hopeless was nothing more than the starting line. It's why they were out today, and why he would continue to badger her until she began to see things his way.

They rode to his mother's favorite place. Richard kept an eagle eye on Grace, even though her mount was used to riding with her specially designed saddle to accommodate her needs.

An hour later they dismounted near a creek under live oak shade trees. Richard and Jack tethered the horses, and then Richard settled Grace on the picnic blanket while Beth and Jack started dishing out the food.

He watched as the beauty of the surroundings finally got Beth to relax. Grace encouraged Beth to start talking about her childhood while he and Richard talked about David's buying trip. Jack admired Beth's easy movements as she got up from the blanket.

"Can I help you?" Jack asked.

"I'm going to pick some flowers to take home with us."

"Take the basket, honey," Grace suggested.

"That's a great idea." Beth took out the remaining containers and slid the handle of the basket over her arm. It was great to see her so excited, and he got out his phone so he could take a picture.

"Oh, you have it bad." Richard laughed.

"What? Everybody needs to have their picture taken in a field of bluebonnets."

"It's true dear," Grace agreed. His mom was a great wingman.

Richard continued to talk, but Jack didn't pay any attention. He watched Beth as she walked away from him in a pair of capris pants that hugged her ass perfectly. Beth's blouse tightened across her breasts when she bent over to pick the first bunch of flowers. There wasn't anything about Beth Hidalgo that didn't call to every one of his senses. He lined up a shot as she placed some flowers into the basket. Her smile was beautiful. He'd send it to Clint for Lydia, and also, save it for himself.

He set down his phone and watched as she enjoyed the afternoon and picked more flowers. Then she reached down and flew backward with a scream. He was up and on the run in a heartbeat. He'd seen it. A snake.

By the time he got there, he was barely aware of the knife in his hand, but he'd cut the head off the rattler and he knelt near Beth. She'd been bitten on her inside upper thigh. *God, right near her femoral artery.*

She was still scrambling backward.

"Is it dead?"

"It's dead. Don't move Beth. I need you to stay still."

"I'm okay. It doesn't hurt too badly."

"When you move the poison has a chance to move around too." She let out a low moan and clamped her hand on her thigh.

"How bad does it hurt? Let me see, okay?"

"Don't be worried. It's not that big of a deal, right?"

"Let me take a look at it. It's a big deal."

She moaned louder. "Okay, maybe you're right. It's beginning to feel like a real big deal. It's starting to hurt."

"I've got you, sweetheart. Stay still while I get a look at this." He heard his dad come up behind him.

"Jack, the chopper is on its way. It'll take her straight to the hospital in San Antonio." He gave Richard a grim nod over his shoulder.

"Beth, I'm going to cut the leg of your pants so I can get to the bite wound, okay?" He didn't wait for her to answer, he just cut. The bite was deep, and already red, and swelling. He touched it, and she gasped in pain.

Dammit, most times you were supposed to give the victim antivenin and not do anything else. But Jack was trained what to do if none was available, or if the venom was going to get into the blood stream.

"Beth, I'm going to have to get some of the venom out." Dazed eyes stared at back at him. Shit, the poison was already beginning to take effect.

"Stick with me, sweetheart. I'm going to suck out some of the poison. This is going to hurt. I'm so sorry, baby."

She looked at him with those big black eyes and nodded. "It's okay, Jack. I trust you. I know you wouldn't hurt me if you didn't have to," she whispered.

He closed his eyes in relief, thankful they had come so far.

He cleaned his knife as best he could then made an incision on her thigh, wincing as she shouted out in pain. She reached out and patted his arm. Amazing. She was offering *him* comfort.

He had to act fast, the bite was too close to the major artery. He gave thanks to Uncle Sam for his training as he sucked out the venom. He hoped against hope he'd gotten most of it. When he heard the helicopter land Beth was unconscious—not a good sign.

They radioed the hospital and bundled her up for the ride into San Antonio. As he looked at her ashen face, Jack realized for the first time how much of his heart Beth Hidalgo owned.

****

"Can you hear me?"

Beth tried to speak, but it was like her tongue was too big for her mouth. She was so tired. It was impossible to open her eyes. The voice faded away.

"Can you tell me where you are?"

Why did they keep asking her questions? She wanted to sleep. She was tired.

"Can you tell me your name?"

"Elsbeth Hidalgo." She could open her eyes for a moment, but they felt swollen as well. She remembered the snake and she shuddered. Where was Jack? She wanted Jack.

"Can you tell me what happened?"

"Snake." Beth shivered.

"That's right. Can you tell me what day you were bitten?"

"Tuesday."

"That's right. What's your name?"

"Elsbeth Hidalgo. Beth. Call me Beth."

"Nurse, I guess we need to correct her name in the system. How are you feeling, Beth?"

"I hurt."

"That's to be expected. Despite your fiancé's quick action, the venom made its way into the artery and spread through your body. You had a very close call. Normally, we don't lose patients to a snake bite, especially when it's treated so fast. Unfortunately, it spread into your bloodstream because it made it into a major artery. You'll be feeling worse side effects than normal."

"Are you thirsty?" the nurse asked.

Beth nodded her head.

The nurse gave her some water. Beth moved her arms and legs. It hurt and it burned to move her right leg.

"Where's Jack?"

"He's been pacing the halls since yesterday," the nurse answered. "We tried to tell him you wouldn't be conscious until today, but he wouldn't leave."

Tears welled, and Beth blinked them back.

"Can he come in?"

"We promised to tell him as soon as you were awake. I want to listen to your heart and make a couple more notes in the system, and then we'll call him in."

"How long will I be in the hospital?"

"We'll see how you're doing in forty-eight to seventy-two hours. Your fiancé assures us you will have round-the-clock care when you leave here. The severity of your symptoms call for bed rest."

Beth stopped herself in time from asking who her fiancé was. Obviously, Jack had claimed to be her intended. He'd explain why, and she didn't want to undo whatever cover story he'd made up.

The doctor placed his stethoscope on her chest. She froze. *Her fiancé. The idea of it made her happy, and that was all kinds of wrong.*

"Are you all right? I need you to relax. Your heart is racing."

"I'm sorry. Can you get Jack?"

"Megan, can you ask for Mr. Preston to come in?"

"Now, do you think you can relax?" The doctor gave her an indulgent smile. Beth took a couple of deep breaths and hoped it slowed her heartbeat.

"Better. Okay, young lady. You need to rest. We'll keep you under observation. We're going to continue to give you medication for the pain. You're lucky, I've seen two severe cases that resulted in partial paralysis. Your young man saved you."

Beth tried to remember what happened, but it was a blur. Only Jack's voice and comforting presence floated in her memories. With him there, she knew it would always be okay.

"Ah, there he is," the doctor said with a smile.

Beth looked up, and the sound of the machines fell away. She was no longer aware of anybody or anything in the hospital room but Jack Preston.

"You scared me, sweetheart." Jack was once again giving her one of his patented warm smiles, but this time, she saw through it. He *was* scared. He wasn't lying.

"Thank you. The doctor said you saved me." He came over and grasped her hand. But it wasn't enough, she wished he was holding her like he had the night of the thunderstorm.

"I should have been walking with you. I wasn't thinking." He turned her hand over and brought her palm to his lips while butterflies took flight in her tummy. She looked around her room and found that they were alone. Then she took a deep breath so she could speak. "Why did you tell them you were my fiancé?" she asked in a whisper.

81

"They were only going to allow family in to see you. A fiancé was considered family." More butterflies. "They told me you were in a lot of pain. How much do you hurt, sweetheart?"

Beth looked down at their hands. He tipped her chin so she was forced to meet his eyes.

"Beth, tell me." He prompted.

"I hurt."

He brushed his thumb over her bottom lip.

"I'm so sorry, I wish I could take the pain for you." She felt tears welling again, and even though she blinked, one leaked out. He brushed it away.

"I'm going to take better care of you when you come home."

"You're only supposed to be protecting me." She gripped his hand even harder.

"Please admit it's more than that. I know you're frightened. But can you be brave enough to admit there's something between us?"

The world stopped. She couldn't catch her breath. She fell into his beautiful blue eyes.

"Beth?" He brushed his thumb against her lips, parting them. "Breathe, baby."

"Yes. Oh, yes, Jack. There's something," she sobbed. "But I'm so scared. What if I can never be what you need?"

"You *are* what I need. You're *who* I need. We have all the time in the world. This is just the beginning. I need to know you'll try." She winced as her leg began to burn and then cramp.

"Ahhh, you're hurting again." Jack bent over and handed her the button so she could release more pain medicine into her I.V.

"I'm going to kiss you now."

So many more butterflies or maybe hummingbirds this time. "Okay," Beth said as she licked her lips.

Jack groaned. Softly, he laid his lips on hers, and she gasped. Taking advantage, his tongue slid along the inside of her lower lip. Teasing and tempting a esponse. She needed more, and he brushed from side to side, stronger as she pushed upward. Jack cupped the back of her head and brought her closer.

His tongue thrust gently, and she shuddered, the sensation unlike any other. More. She closed her eyes and sucked him in, savoring his taste and his masculine heat. Her breasts grew taut, her nipples beaded against his chest. Beth heard him make a sound of approval as he pulled her against him. She heard a whimper and realized it was her.

****

The woman was like aged whiskey and sunflowers. She was fast becoming his everything. Jack forced himself to pull back when he heard her whimper. She was ill.

"No." She lifted her arms to wrap around his neck and groaned.

"Oh, Beth, I know you're hurting. Don't move your arms like that."

"I didn't want you to stop." Her black eyes glowed. Her lips were swollen from their kiss. Jack had to fight down his reaction. *For God's sake, she's in a hospital bed, Preston!* It didn't seem to matter; he was going to end up leaving the room with a hard-on.

"We'll talk when you come back home. In the meantime, get some rest. I bet the medicine is making you sleepy."

She yawned. "Jack," her voice came out slurred. "I like how you call the ranch home. It makes it sound like it's my home, too."

His gut clenched. He looked in wonder at this woman who he'd only just kissed for the first time.

"When you're better, Beth, we're going to need to talk about the future."

"I know." She yawned again, her eyes blinking slowly, a sure sign she was close to sleep. "It's good

I'm leaving soon. I still don't think this can work. I'm broken, and you deserve so much better."

"I never want to hear you say you're broken again." She jerked at the heat in his voice, her eyes wide.

"Sweetheart, I'm sorry." He cupped her cheek. "You've been through a trauma, and you're working your way through it. I think you're one of the bravest women I've ever met next to my mom. I'm going to have to tell you my story one day so you know I understand where you're coming from."

"But…"

"No buts." He pressed a gentle kiss to her lips until she was asleep.

"Sweet dreams, my Beth."

****

Jack looked at the display on his phone. He wasn't surprised to see it was the number Clint had provided.

"Preston."

"How is she? Is she awake? Can I talk to her?" Jack had spoken to Lydia only twice before and never heard her so frantic.

"Lydia, she's going to be fine. The doctors say she's going to make a complete recovery."

"Thank God. Can I talk to her?"

"I just left her. She was asleep." There was a long pause, and he could hear her disappointment through the phone.

"I promise the next time she wakes up the first thing I'll have her do will be to call you, okay?"

"Do you promise?"

"I promise."

"Thank you. Thank you so much for my sister's life." Jack felt himself hunch over at her words.

"You're welcome. She'll call you tomorrow." He hung up the phone and looked at his parents.

His mother used her cane to stand up, waving Richard off when he tried to help her. Jack went over to her.

"You need to go to the hotel now."

"Mom, she could wake up again," Jack protested.

"If she does, we'll be here. We've had a full night's sleep. You haven't."

"I'm staying."

"Son, you're worrying your mother. At least go take a shower and a nap," Richard suggested. Jack looked between the two of them and nodded.

Chapter Seven

"Have you told her how you feel?"

"It would scare her even more if I told her I think I'm falling in love with her. In the hospital, I asked her to consider the future, and she said stupid shit about being broken."

His mom just left Beth's room. They'd brought her back to the ranch two days earlier, and it was going to take a bit of time before she was done recuperating. His mom made sure she finished some of the soup Rosa made for her. Now, she was back in the great room staring at her son.

"You know feeling unworthy is part of PTSD, right?"

"I know. I'm not pushing too hard. At least, I don't think I am. But, Mom, I can't stand the fact she thinks less of herself." He brought the ottoman over and gently lifted her legs so they rested on top of it.

"Richard had to contend with the same thing when he first met me. I didn't think I would ever be able to have a relationship after what your father had done."

"I thought he had to convince you *he* was good enough, and he wouldn't hurt you." Jack thought back to his childhood years when Richard was courting his mother.

"No, he had to help me see I was good enough."

Jack sat in the chair next to his mother's and really looked at her. It had been a long time since they had talked about the years they spent with his biological father.

"Do you still think about him? Do you still have nightmares?"

"Do you, Jack?"

He stopped himself from immediately giving a negative response.

"I was on a mission last year. I won't go into the details."

"I'm glad. I try not to worry too much when you're overseas, but I do. I always pray for your safe return."

"I appreciate it. Anyway, we rescued a kid. He just turned thirteen, the son of an American oil executive, and he'd been kidnapped and held for ransom. The kidnapper was a sadist."

His mother rested her hand on his knee and squeezed.

"The boy, Kevin, is doing better now."

"You've been having nightmares?" she said knowingly.

"Yeah. It brought back those years with him." Even now, a trained Navy SEAL and his dreams could take him back to the scared six-year-old whose father was such a monster and had held all the power.

"But, Mom, I don't get it, why does Beth feel damaged? Why did you?" Looking at the beautiful woman in front of him, he couldn't imagine her thinking of herself as broken. As 'less than'.

"Didn't you? Isn't it why you had to ride the wildest horses? Drive the fastest car? Win every fight against the biggest kids in school? Become a SEAL? Weren't you trying to prove you weren't that defenseless boy?"

"To begin with, yes, but halfway through college, I wanted to start helping others. I already knew I was the baddest thing out there, and I wanted to use it in defense of others. But, Mom, I never felt I was unlovable or somehow not worthy, only powerless."

"I think the type of touch Beth and I endured is somehow so degrading that you feel defiled. I don't know how many times I rubbed myself raw in the shower, trying to get clean. I couldn't imagine anyone else thinking I was good enough."

Jack blinked back tears, he'd had no idea his mother ever felt like that.

"Then, there was the fact I didn't think I could ever handle a man's touch again. It took a long time for Richard to convince me otherwise."

"Jesus, Mom. I wish I'd known, I could've helped."

"It wasn't something you could have helped with. I thank God for Richard coming into my life. Into our lives. I think Beth is going to ultimately feel the same way about you."

"She lets me hold her. And holding Beth is better than anything else I've done with other women." Jack remembered how soft and right she felt in his arms, and he ached to have her there again.

"Then she's definitely the one."

"I think so too, but we still have a lot of hurdles to cross. I want to help her, and coax her but not pressure her. I'm not sure I know the difference."

"Oh honey, I trust you. You have great instincts."

****

Sometimes, it felt like Boone was the only one who understood Beth.

"Isn't that right, boy?" The dog pushed closer as she sat on the top step of the porch. Her emotions had been up and down for the last two days. She was still replaying the kiss in the hospital. Sometimes, she felt like there might be a future with Jack. But most of the time she knew there couldn't be.

Boone whined. She'd been squeezing him too tightly.

"I'm sorry, boy. I can't seem to do anything right."

"I wouldn't say that's true." Jack had been silent this time when he had stepped onto the porch.

"Are you okay, Beth?"

"Sure." She didn't look up, preferring to keep her face hidden in the scruff of Boone's neck.

"Why don't you think you can do anything right?"

"Because I can't." Her fingers dug into the dog's fur, and once again, he whined. She let go of him and he darted down the stairs. *Yep, nothing right, I can't even keep the dog by my side.*

"Beth, you're an amazing woman. I think you've had a hell of a lot to deal with. It takes a while to heal."

She laughed and then winced. She hated the bitter sound that came out of her mouth.

"I think you need a hug."

"Not even Boone wanted a hug from me."

"Look up, sweetheart, there's a rabbit in the garden. You're never going to compete."

"Seriously, Jack, I'm not good company."

"Let me make my own decision." He sat beside her, and his warmth felt good even though she didn't want it to.

"Beth, you know this takes time."

"I've resigned myself to it never getting better. It's too high a mountain to climb." She pulled her knees up and rested her head on her crossed arms.

"Mom thought that. Hell, I thought that myself too."

She peeked at him through her lashes and saw him gazing off into the distance.

"Is this about your real dad?"

"It was bad. I don't know everything that happened between Mom and Dad. From some of what she's told me, it was awful." Beth rested one hand on his shoulder.

"She tried to protect me as best she could. Dad threatened to kill me if she tried to leave. She didn't have a job or family...I remember always feeling helpless. I wanted to help protect her. I hated feeling so defenseless. So weak."

"Exactly!" *Jack did understand!*

"All I can tell you is for me and my mom it got better."

"Your mom is stronger than I am."

"I think the world of my mom. But you, Elsbeth Hildago, are extraordinary."

She looked into Jack's deep blue eyes and saw nothing but sincerity. He made her *want* to climb mountains.

"Come on, what say you and I go visit the horses. You're not up for riding yet, but they've missed you."

"No, they haven't."

"You've claimed the heart of damn near every creature on this ranch." He stood and brushed off the back of his jeans, affording her a fine view of his ass. He turned in time to see her admiring glance. He gave her a slow grin as he held out his hand.

"Let's go to the barn." She blushed as she took his hand.

Midway across the yard, he draped his arm over her shoulder and she leaned into him.

Chapter Eight

"Jack, we have a major fucking problem." His heart beat fast for a moment, and then returned to its normal rhythm. Now was the time for calm.

"What's the problem, Mason?"

"Somehow it got into the system that Elsbeth Hildago was a patient at the San Antonio hospital."

Jack didn't say anything. It shouldn't have been possible, but obviously, it was. No use crying over spilled milk. Instead, he needed to focus on how to contain the damage.

"What options are you considering, Sir?"

"Clint wants her to go with him and Lydia."

"That's a negative. We wanted them separate for a reason, it's still valid now."

"That's what I think, but her cover is blown in San Antonio. What's more, you're on file as her fiancé. We need her transferred to somewhere new and split from you, too."

95

"That's a negative too, Sir."

"You don't have a choice, soldier. It's an order."

"You don't understand the situation. This is the woman I'm going to marry. Where she goes, I go."

"I beg your pardon?"

"You heard me. She doesn't know it yet, so keep it to yourself, but I intend to marry Beth."

"You're a stubborn son of a bitch, Preston." Jack heard the other man sigh. "Okay, I hear you. We'll make this work. You and Beth will stay together."

"Thanks, Mason. You won't regret this. I'll protect her with my life."

Jack brushed his thumb over the blank screen of his phone. It was an earth-shattering moment to realize you were so in love you intended to marry someone. But there it was. He intended to spend the rest of his life with Beth, and nobody was going to come between them. Except maybe Beth. He loved her so much that if this truly wasn't what she wanted he'd step back. It would kill him, but he would do it.

But he would bet anything if she wasn't in love with him now, it was a near thing. What was stopping her was her fear of intimacy and failing. But he would do everything in his power to make sure those fears would not stop her from having her dreams come true. He had a goal. SEALs worked well with goals. SEALs achieved their goals. Jack smiled.

****

Two hours later he got the call from Clint with the plan. He and Beth would be going to the Los Angeles area.

"It'll be close enough to San Diego that we'll be able to rotate in plenty of back-up. You can get lost in L.A. County. In the meantime, Lydia and I'll be in San Diego."

"You're bringing the sisters that close together? Is it wise?"

"We want to keep them close together so there will be plenty of back-up for protection."

"Where exactly will Beth and I be?"

"Santa Monica." Jack wasn't too familiar with the city, but he'd been there. "Is this a safe house the US Marshals are providing?"

"Hell no. It's another SEAL—his girlfriend's house. She's going to stay with him. It's not as isolated as your ranch, and it's not going to be as easy to protect, but we have the personnel."

Jack mulled over what Clint told him and realized he wasn't being told everything. "You can't be stretched that thin. Where are her parents being stashed?"

Clint chuckled. "I like you, Jack."

"Cut the shit."

"They're going to be close by too. They've moved the trial venue to California," Clint explained.

"Doesn't it have to stay in the same state?"

"Apparently not since it's a federal case. Too much publicity and too many threats in Texas, so they moved it to LA."

"Why the hell didn't you say so in the first place?"

"Because we're still arguing with the Marshals. Right now the girl's parents are still with Finn in the frozen tundra of Middle America. The Marshals are demanding for the next move they are in charge of their care."

"That's a bad move. The Marshals were infiltrated before, what makes them think they won't be again?" Jack asked.

"Because they would work with a small team in California."

"Will Beth be able to see her parents? Will she be able to see Lydia?"

"Hell Jack, until I'm satisfied that the Marshals have cleaned house, there is only going to be contact between Lydia and Beth."

Jack sighed in relief. He was in total agreement.

"But Preston, I have a question for you."

"Shoot."

"Does Beth know your intentions?"

Jack took a deep breath. "You mean what I said to Mason?"

"That'd be what I'm talking about."

"I didn't know it's how I felt until the words came out of my mouth. So no, she doesn't know. When I've tried to broach any kind of relationship she shuts down. She doesn't think she's capable. It's my job to prove to her otherwise."

"Gotchya. Let me tell you, these Hidalgo women are worth it."

Jack grinned. "So, when do we leave?"

"Tonight."

"I better go tell Beth."

****

Something was up. Jack had been holed up in his father's study for the last three hours, and he'd missed their riding lesson. It was the second one they were going to have since she had gotten home from the hospital, and she knew only something important would have made him miss it. She was nervous, so she was out in the garden with Boone.

The dog barked his welcome, and she looked over her shoulder to see Jack walking over towards her with a strained smile. She gave a tentative smile in return and stood brushing the dirt off her jeans.

"Sweetheart, I have some good news and a change in plans."

"So no bad news?" She knew Jack, he would try to protect her. He wouldn't want to worry her. There was some bad news hidden somewhere.

"The good news is you're going to be able to see Lydia sooner than we thought."

"Is she all right?"

"She's fine. They've decided to move the trial from Texas to California. So all of you are going to be moving. Lydia is going to San Diego, your parents are going to Los Angeles and we're going to Santa Monica."

"I'm still not good with the geography of the United States, but aren't all of those places in California?"

"Yes."

"I thought we're supposed to be kept far apart. This doesn't make sense."

Jack took a deep breath.

"What aren't you telling me?"

"It's because they can keep more Navy personnel guarding all of you if you're in the Southern California area. They wouldn't put you in harm's way. If they say it's okay for all of you to be in the same area until the trial, then it's okay."

"Can I talk to Lydia today?"

"Better than that. You'll get to see her tomorrow."

He was trying too hard, and Beth understood why. She appreciated his efforts, but she was tired of it. If she didn't start standing up for herself, she was always going to be treated like a delicate little girl. Stepping forward, she rested one hand on his broad chest and pushed a wayward strand of straw-colored hair from his forehead.

"Tell me the truth, I'm a big girl, I can handle it. Why do we have to leave the ranch?"

He took in another deep breath.

"Somehow the people at the hospital found out your real name. It's now in the hospital records that Beth Hidalgo was a patient there, not Beth Ochoa." She reeled backward, but he caught both of her hands.

"What? What is it Beth?"

"It's my fault. When I first woke up, they asked me my name, and I told them my real name. I did this Jack. I messed up. *Madre de Dios.*"

She turned her head away in shame.

"Look at me Beth, it's not a problem, we adapt."

"It is a problem. I am an *idiota.*"

"Stop it. You're not an idiot. You'd been unconscious. You were in a lot of pain, and the doctor was asking you questions. Chances are I would have done the same thing."

She stopped and looked at him. He looked sincere.

"Really?"

"Really. I've had drugs for wounds and they've made me disoriented. It's tough to fight the effects."

"You've been wounded?" Beth asked, zeroing in on the most important thing he'd said—at least to her.

"Just a couple of times and they weren't bad. I've been lucky."

Beth thought it would be rude to ask what happened or where he was injured, but she wanted to know.

"We leave tomorrow?"

"No, Beth, we leave immediately. Your location has been compromised. Dad is going to take mom on a vacation for the next couple of weeks just to be on the safe side. She and Rosa are inside packing." Jack let go of one of her hands and brushed her bottom lip where she was biting it.

"Sweetheart, you're biting so hard you'll bleed."

"I've ruined everything. I need to go in and say good-bye."

"I'll go with you, and you haven't ruined anything. Mom is over the moon at the idea of a vacation with dad. She said she's been trying to get him away from work for two years. She's going to kiss you."

"Mmm hmm." Jack tugged her hand and drew her towards the house. That was the thing about him. He was always on her side, and she was going to be the same way. She pulled back.

"Everything's fine." He stepped forward and wrapped his arms around her. Every good intention washed away. He deserved better than her. He needed someone who wasn't broken. Here he was, having to clean up her screw-up. But she couldn't resist the lure of his hug, and she snuggled in.

He smelled so good, like leather, soap, and a scent that was just Jack. He was so big compared to her, but she always felt safe when he was near. She relaxed for the moment and basked in his strength, enjoying it while she could. Soon enough they'd have to part.

****

"Shoo. I want to talk to Beth alone." Beth loved the look of warm indulgence on Jack's face.

"Yes, Mom. But remember she and I have to leave in the next hour."

"Well the sooner you leave, the sooner she and I will be done. Now shoo." He chuckled and left.

Rosa already left Grace's bedroom, so it was just the two of them.

"Come and sit down, honey." She patted a spot on the bed beside her, and Beth sat down. She had no idea what Jack's mother might have to say, but she was ready for anything.

"I can't tell you how impressed I am with you." *Well, anything but that*.

Beth stared at Jack's mother.

"I'm serious. You experienced a terrible trauma, you've been on the run, and then there was the damn snake, and yet you've kept it all together. You're a remarkable young woman. I only see one problem."

Here it comes.

"You don't know how special you are."

"Grace, I don't think you're seeing things clearly. I still have nightmares. I'm still scared of so much. I'm the one who told my real name and now we all have to leave. I've messed up things badly and I'm like a scared little bunny."

Grace laughed. "That's exactly what I mean. Real courage is doing things despite being scared. You haven't hidden away and stayed in your bedroom. You have dealt with your fears and interacted with my husband and David, even though they reminded you of your attackers."

"Thank you, but you're giving me too much credit." Grace nodded as if she had made a decision.

"Has Jack told you my background? Did he tell you why I walk with a cane?"

"He told me about his father, but he didn't tell me about the cane."

105

"Jack's biological father was very abusive. He beat me. He hurt Jack sometimes too, and I wasn't able to protect him."

Beth clenched her fists. She hated the thought of either Grace or Jack having been hurt, but especially Jack as a small child. Grace placed her hand over Beth's.

"I know. I know. But Jack was so strong, so stoic."

"Stoic?" She didn't understand the word.

"He never showed he was scared. Sometimes I think it would have been better if he had, it would have calmed Burt down. Instead, Jack would just stare him down. It would infuriate my husband."

"What happened then? What happened to you? How did you end up injured?"

"One night he'd been drinking. I think he'd gotten into an argument while he was out, and lost some money. He came home so angry and needed to take it out on someone. I'd made dinner, but he didn't like it. It had dried out because he'd come home so late."

Grace gulped. She looked down and picked at the quilt covering the bed.

"It's okay, you don't have to tell me."

"You're a sweet girl. I want you to see we're not all that different. That you *can* make a life for yourself

106

no matter what happens. You're starting to, but you can have so much more."

Beth's laugh sounded hollow even to her. She and Grace couldn't be more different. This woman was vibrant. Everyone gravitated towards her. Hell, Beth couldn't even take classes at a university.

"I can see you don't agree with me, but let me finish my story. Burt came home that night and he pushed me down and kicked me. He kept kicking me. Jack ran to the neighbor's house and got help, and they called the police. I was passed out on the floor by the time they arrived. Someone told me Burt was calmly sitting at the table eating his supper."

Beth could picture it. Her family lived in a very bad neighborhood when she was young, and there had been a lot of violence. Domestic violence had not been uncommon. "What happened next?"

"Burt was sent to prison, and I was hospitalized. Jack was sent to foster care for three months while I recovered since I had no family to take him. When I got out, we had to live in a shelter. It was over two years before I could really talk to anyone, let alone a man. That's why I'm so impressed with you."

"You're kidding, right? Our stories are nothing alike. You went through so much more than I ever have."

"Really, Beth? My gut tells me you've been scared longer than you've let on. I think it's remarkable that you've come so far so fast. I want you to take it a little further. Trust my son. He's a good man."

Now it was Beth's turn to twist the fabric of the quilt. How could this woman see things so much more clearly than even her family?

"I can't really talk about it."

"Eventually, you'll need to talk to someone. You can't carry these types of burdens alone. Trust me, I know. In the meantime, I wanted you to know how much I admire you and believe in you."

That was it. Beth burst into tears.

"Oh, honey."

Grace cradled her close to her heart. Not even with her mother had she felt so understood and cared for. Too often *she* needed to be the caretaker.

"Just let it out."

Beth thought about what was said at the shack where they'd been held prisoner, and the visits at her father's office when she'd helped out. She was scared. It'd been fine when they didn't know where she was when she'd been under an assumed name, but now... She pushed out of Grace's arms.

"When are you leaving?"

"Tomorrow. Richard and I are going to a friend's house in Florida."

Beth wiped her eyes.

"Leave today." Grace must have seen something in her face.

"All right, we will. But Beth, I'm serious, you need to trust my son. He's good at what he does. He can help you, but only if he knows everything that's going on. I've been in your shoes. Keeping secrets will get you hurt, maybe even killed."

"I'll think about what you said. But I'm probably making this all up in my head. I overreact to things. My parents say I need to be more like Lydia."

"I've never met your sister. But I stand by what I said. Don't doubt yourself, Beth. Tell Jack what you're thinking. Trust your instincts."

"Maybe I will."

Grace rubbed her hip. "Can you go over to my dresser and get that blue box?"

Beth saw a small jeweler's box. "This one?"

"Yes. Bring it to me." Beth handed it to her.

"No, no. It's for you. Open it."

Beth frowned. But at Grace's insistent expression, she opened the box and saw a beautiful heart shaped opal necklace. Grace pulled out a similar one from beneath her blouse.

"Richard gave me this soon after we met. It was his grandmother's. She was from Australia. It's supposed to help the wearer reach their highest potential. I don't know if I believe that, but Edna managed the family cattle ranch after her husband died. I know after I started wearing it I believed in myself more. It could just be the power of suggestion. But I wanted you to have one too."

Beth stared at the beautiful blue stone flashing with hints of green and red. She'd never seen anything so pretty.

"Here, let me help you put it on."

"I can't take this."

"I had it made for you. You have to take it."

Beth looked into Grace's determined blue eyes and saw she was not going to win this argument. She touched the beautiful stone set in a silver heart. She wanted this necklace. She took it out of the box and handed it to Grace.

"Lift up your hair."

Grace did the clasp, and Beth looked in the mirror. She couldn't help but smile. There was a knock on the door and Jack walked in.

"Beth, you've got to pack."

"Just one last hug," Grace insisted.

"Yes." Beth smiled.

Jack shook his head at the women. He waited, and then he gave his mom a hug as well.

"Be safe Jack, and take care of Beth."

"You know it."

"I do."

Chapter Nine

Beth packed two suitcases, and Jack packed a duffle bag. They took the helicopter to San Antonio and met a man who handed them envelopes with new IDs.

"How is this possible so fast?" Beth looked bewildered.

"Mason's team has some serious connections."

"But the US Marshals took a couple of days to set things up," Beth said as they were driven to the airport by the same man.

"Miss, there are some heavy brass working on this mission. Lieutenant Gault is getting everything he wants. He intends to keep all of you safe."

"Just sit back and enjoy the ride, so to speak." Jack stroked her arm in comfort. He knew everything was going pretty fast. All he wanted was to get her settled into their new location in Santa Monica. The faster she could see Lydia, the better she'd feel.

They were on the plane before she could think, which was his plan to begin with. LAX was a mess, as always, and why he usually flew into San Diego

Airport. It might be an International Airport, but it felt more local. LAX was just crazy. When he said as much to Beth, she laughed.

"You need to fly out of the Mexico City International Airport. Especially when you are on the run. Then you'll see crazy."

"Good point. You win." He could still see she was anxious, she had a habit of clenching her fists. He kept his arm around her while they were at baggage claim, with one eye on the carousel and the other on the door. Darius Lane and Drake Avery walked in. They were the men from the Midnight Delta SEAL team he'd been waiting for. It was easy to recognize them from the pictures Mason had sent in an e-mail. Jack breathed a sigh of relief but it was short-lived. He hugged Beth closer and worried how she'd handle being surrounded by two more large men.

They approached while scanning the baggage claim area. Jack spotted their luggage as the men stepped forward.

"Beth! You look beautiful, beautiful!" Drake pulled her out of Jack's arms and immersed her in a hug. She immediately stiffened and struggled backward.

"Jesus Avery, how fucking dense are you?" Darius pulled Drake back, and Beth fell into Jack's arms.

"But...I don't understand. Blondie's holding her."

113

"Did you even ask? No, you just assumed. It's a wonder you don't get punched on a regular basis." Darius shook his head in exasperation.

"Dare, I don't need this shit." Drake turned towards Beth and took note of her tentative smile.

"Honey, I'm so sorry. I saw you cuddled up to the Viking and thought you were better. After all, he's a freaking giant."

The idiot just kept putting his foot in his mouth. "Back off, Avery," Jack growled.

"Hey, I know Beth. She and I have quite the history. We spent long sultry nights under the stars. Beth, tell the man."

Now the dumb shit had two feet in his mouth. *Amazing*. Before Jack could say anything, Beth giggled.

"It's okay, Jack. Drake is Drake."

"You better believe it. And I'm going to be the first man who will beat the ever loving shit out of anyone who harms one hair on your head. You have my number don't you, gorgeous?"

Jack stared in disbelief. He looked at Beth and saw her look of resignation.

"Drake. Shut the fuck up," Darius said as he pushed him aside and stepped forward. "Hey Beth, how are you doing?"

Beth took a deep breath and smiled at Darius.

"Hi. I see Drake hasn't changed."

"Not a bit. But, if his phone doesn't answer you call me." Darius winked, and she laughed. "You look good, the ranch must have agreed with you."

"Mostly it did, except for the rattlesnake."

Jack grabbed the luggage, and Darius grabbed one of Beth's suitcases.

"I heard about the snake," Darius said, as he gave her an encouraging smile.

"That was damn good work, Preston," Drake said.

"He saved my life," Beth said, as she leaned into Jack. Now she was back in his arms he could appreciate the men's concern.

"That's the reason he's getting a pass," Drake said.

"Oh can it already," Jack said shaking his head as they exited the terminal.

Darius laughed. "Seems like Jack has your number, Drake."

"Maybe," Drake admitted.

"The car is out this way." The men surrounded Beth as they exited the terminal. Darius assured them it wasn't far to Santa Monica, but it seemed to take forever.

"This traffic is hellish. I thought San Diego was bad," Drake complained. "We've only gone seven miles. Aren't there some side streets we could have taken?"

"Stop your bitching. We're committed to this route. We'll be there shortly," Darius replied.

"I knew I should have driven," Drake muttered.

"I wanted us to get there in one piece."

"At least, I don't drive like somebody's grandmother," Drake scoffed.

Jack listened to the banter in the front and watched Beth looking out the window. She seemed lost in her own world.

Finally, they arrived at a little bungalow-style house. There were two men, obviously military, waiting for them. This time, Beth turned to him with trepidation.

"I know them, they were sent by my lieutenant. They're currently in training. Trust me, you'll like them, they're good guys.

"We know them too," Darius assured her. He got out of the car and opened Beth's door. Jack followed her, and she immediately sidled up to him. He liked it. They walked up to the front door.

"Gentlemen, please introduce yourselves."

"Petty Officer Third Class, Lou Griggs, Ma'am."

"Petty Officer Second Class, Mike Ingram, Ma'am."

Beth looked at him.

"This is Beth Llamos. She's who you're going to be guarding. I don't want anyone you don't personally know, or who hasn't been cleared by one of us to be let into this house. Am I clear?"

"Clear, Sir." The men answered in unison.

"Do you have the keys to the house?"

"Right here." Griggs handed the keys to Jack. "We checked inside, it's fine, Sir." Jack nodded and motioned to Darius, who held Beth back as Jack let himself inside. The house was nice and homey. He checked every room, closet, and hidey hole. Finally, he went back outside and nodded. Darius escorted Beth inside.

Jack watched as Beth looked around and gave a slow and delighted smile. "This is lovely."

"This is my buddy's girlfriend's house," Mike said. "Her grandmother used to live here. Anyway, she stocked the refrigerator, and she said to tell you she changed the sheets."

Beth's smile turned into a frown.

"Where's she going to be? I didn't mean to put anyone out."

"Are you kidding? Jerry is happy as a clam. He's been trying to get Claudia to stay with him for over a year. Now they get to do a test run before he proposes. Everything's cool."

"Come on, Beth, let's take a tour."

"We're going to take off. We'll see you tomorrow down in San Diego. In the meantime, Mike and Lou will be stationed outside." Darius and Drake took her hand in a gentle shake goodbye.

After the door had closed, Beth stood in the middle of the open floor plan living space and stared at him. "I don't know what to do," she said.

"Just take it easy. Tomorrow's a big day, and you'll get to see Lydia."

"I'm too excited to take it easy." Beth laughed, then hugged herself and practically danced over to the kitchen counter. She picked up a pear from the bowl on the counter that separated the living room from the kitchen.

"Look how fresh these are." She opened her mouth to say something else and then yawned. After she was done, she attempted to finish her comment but instead yawned again.

"That's it. Bedtime, little girl." Jack picked up her two suitcases. "Follow me."

"I can't believe how tired I am."

He could. He waited for her at the start of the small hallway. "It's the door at the end. The one on the left is the guest bathroom."

"Which one is your bedroom?"

"I'm bunking on the couch."

"But it's too small," she protested.

"It's fine. If I'm too uncomfortable, I'll sleep on the floor. Trust me, it's better than one hundred percent of my assignments."

"Assignments?" Jack looked at her face as he put the suitcase on the bed. He knew he'd screwed up, and pulled her into his arms.

"You're not an assignment. You're a joy. I meant compared to sleeping in the desert, sleeping outside your door is an honor and a little bit of hell." He smiled to make sure she understood he was teasing.

"I'm so anxious. I mean not only will I get to see Lydia but next week Papa testifies. Soon everything will be over with."

119

Jack took a step forward and cupped her cheeks. "Not everything. I'm not letting you go, Beth."

"Jack," she breathed out.

He put a finger over her lips.

"Dammit, I shouldn't have said that. You go to sleep. Just know you're safe, and someone cares deeply about you, okay?"

"But, I don't want you hurt."

"I'm a big boy. The most important thing is your happiness. I know I need to back off. Now, you get some sleep. Remember, tomorrow is a big day. It's reunion day." A smile suffused her face.

"You're right. But, we're going to talk about you and me."

"Such a brave girl. Now go to sleep."

"Yes, Sir." She grinned, and he shut the door behind him.

Chapter Ten

Nothing went quite as expected. The next day, when Jack and Beth went over to the duplex where Clint and Lydia were staying, they found a very sober Lydia. She tried to hide it, but it was obvious something was wrong.

"Lydia, are you okay?"

"I'm fine. I'm so glad you're finally here and we're together again. The Marshals even said they'll bring Mama and Papa here very soon."

Lydia offered Jack and Beth something to drink as they sat in the living room of the pretty home.

"I don't want anything to drink, Lydia. I want to know what's wrong. Tell me," Beth demanded.

Jack put his hand over Beth's and looked at her sister. "It's really good to finally meet you, Lydia."

"I'm so sorry, Jack," Beth said. "I should have introduced you first thing."

"It's okay. But the real problem is Clint isn't here. He's been deployed, hasn't he?" he asked Lydia in a gentle voice.

She looked at Jack with shiny eyes and nodded. Beth crossed over to the chair where Lydia was sitting, sat on the arm, and gave her sister a hug.

"Oh Lyd, you should have told me first thing. When did he leave?"

"Yesterday morning, at oh-God-awful-o'clock. Sophia Anderson, Mason's fiancée came over here for a visit and spent the night." Lydia bit her lip. Normally Lydia was not a crier, except when she'd had pneumonia. Beth hated seeing her so upset.

"I'm sorry, this was supposed to be our big reunion and instead I'm a shit companion." Lydia stood and pulled Beth into her arms and gave her the big hug of welcome Beth had been envisioning for well over a month.

"I've missed you so much, Lydia."

"Me too, baby sister." Then both women started to laugh and cry at the same time.

Lydia turned to Jack, who was still sitting on the sofa watching with a bemused expression on his face.

"So you're Jack Preston, the man who saved my sister's life. I can't thank you enough." She went over and stood in front of him with her arms outstretched. Jack stood, and he towered over Lydia. Beth was used to his size, so it was a bit of a shock to realize how big the man was in comparison to her sister. She smothered a laugh because Lydia was actually a little taller than she was.

"He's a big one."

"Damn, can you still read my mind?" Beth demanded good-naturedly.

"It's one of the perks of being the oldest."

"You're as beautiful as your sister," Jack said.

"Something tells me you're actually a little biased towards Beth," Lydia teased as she stepped back from Jack. Jack's face flushed.

"Maybe a little. Your sister is a very special lady."

"Yes, she is." Lydia glanced over her shoulder at Beth and gave her a smile. She turned back to Jack. "So you're a SEAL too, huh?"

"Yes, Ma'am. I mean Lydia, I guess saying ma'am is a Navy habit and it's hard to break." Beth noted Lydia's sad expression again, and Jack must have as well.

"Why don't I take you two pretty ladies to lunch? I know a lot of great places here in the San Diego area. Then you can tell me what it was like growing up in

Mexico. I can also practice my Spanish with two natives."

"That would be really nice. Let me get my purse." Lydia gave him a grateful smile. While she went to the bedroom, Beth hugged him.

"What's this for?"

"I think you're wonderful."

"If offering to take two beautiful women to lunch gets me a hug from you, I'll be doing it every day for the rest of my life." He looked at her, and for a moment she thought she might get kissed, but then she heard Lydia coming down the hall and the moment was gone.

"Come along ladies, your chariot awaits."

As they made their way outside, Jack looked around and saw Terry and Chris and gave them a nod.

"Lydia, where are your guards?"

"Frank's over there. His partner's wife is sick today so I told him to go home."

Jack's face darkened. "Why don't the two of you head over to the SUV? I'll be there in a sec." He headed towards the car where Frank was seated. Frank sat up straight and looked worried. Beth thought he should be.

****

"I had a great time today, thank you so much," Beth said as they got home.

Jack tipped his chin to the two men stationed outside the bungalow as they made their way inside.

"I did too. Your sister is as nice as I imagined she'd be."

"She is, isn't she?" Beth headed towards the kitchen. She was full of excited energy and it was a joy to watch.

God, she was gorgeous.

She was holding a coffee cup and turned around to look at him.

"What?"

"Hmm?"

"You're staring."

"You're beautiful."

"I'm not really, but I like it when you say I am. Now, is it too late for you to have coffee? You always seem to drink it no matter how late it is. I'll brew you some, but I'm having tea."

Jack shuddered. "Coffee. Definitely coffee." He watched in fascination as she hummed, and then started to softly sing a song in Spanish.

"What song is that?"

"Oh." Beth laughed. "I didn't even realize I was singing. Lydia and I used to drive Mama crazy with this song. It was popular about ten years ago—a boy band. I actually don't like it all that much to tell you the truth, but it brings back happy memories."

Beth handed Jack his cup of coffee and got the milk and sugar for her tea.

"What's the age difference between you and your sister?"

"Three and a half years. She's the smart one." Jack watched as she stirred, taking in her relaxed expression. Beth meant exactly what she said. *Interesting.*

"Tell me more about Lydia. What was it like growing up with her?"

"It was great. She looked out for me. She was fierce. You would've thought with how beautiful she was she would've been one of the popular girls, but she was a computer nerd." Beth looked at him with a huge grin. "I was lucky to have her. She's always protected me." With those few words, Beth was no longer smiling. Jack knew she was lost in a jungle.

"Hey sweetheart, let's focus on today, shall we?"

"Yes, you're right. I know Lydia's upset because Clint was deployed, but I'm so happy she has him. She deserves him...well he deserves her." She stopped and looked at him, her eyes sparkling. "They deserve each other, in a good way. They're good people," she said with a long sigh.

"You deserve it too, sweetheart." Her smile lost its sparkle, and she looked at him with a resigned expression. "Don't look at me like that. I think *we* deserve each other." He stepped closer so their bodies touched. Her eyes widened, and her breath quickened, but he saw no fear in her eyes. What he saw was shy interest. He smiled as he bent close and parted her lips with his.

It took a long moment, but eventually her eyes fluttered shut. Jack wrapped one arm around her back and sifted the other through her hair until he could tilt her head just so. His eyes drifted shut as he took the kiss to a whole new level. He tasted the heady flavor that was Beth. He shifted his knee and she moved so her legs surrounded it, and her core pushed against his upper thigh. He moved it upwards and her fingernails bit into his biceps, and she nipped at his lips.

They were little advances, but coming from Beth, it made him hard as a rock. He slipped his hand under her blouse and luxuriated in the smooth skin of her tummy. He loved how round and soft she was, she felt so good to him, and she'd feel like heaven

127

underneath him. He pressed harder with his thigh, and he heard her moan.

He traced his fingers along her ribcage, and he felt her breath catch. She arched further into the kiss her tongue tangling with his. His heart began to gallop, but he kept all of his responses in check knowing this was new to her. He slid his hand up her side, then around to her front, and smiled as he felt the cotton of the serviceable bra she was wearing. No lace for his girl. She twisted and moaned.

He gently cupped her breast, loving the feel of the warm weight in his palm, and the way she shifted against his hand. It took a moment for him to realize she wasn't moving towards him, but away. *Fuck!*

He broke off the kiss and looked at her, but saw only a slight bit of panic. Thank the Lord.

"Beth, it's all right. It stops now."

She sucked in a deep breath. "I'm sorry. I wasn't expecting you to touch me there." Her big black eyes held remorse and sorrow. "I told you this wouldn't work between the two of us."

"Sweetheart, I just took you by surprise. You said so yourself, you weren't expecting it."

She looked at him with a considering expression. "Did you like everything else?" he asked.

"Yes, but," her voice trailed off.

"Do you trust me? I mean *really* trust me?"

"Yes."

He'd known the answer, and he knew the answer to the next couple of questions, but *she* had to know them.

"Do you think I'd ever physically harm you?"

"God no!"

"Before me, did you ever think you'd want to hold a man's hand?"

"No."

"Hug a man?"

"No."

"Sit in his lap?"

"No." Her eyes began to sparkle.

"Kiss one?"

"You know the answer."

"Tell me anyway," he coaxed.

"No, before you I never wanted to kiss a man."

"Have you enjoyed doing those things with me?"

"Oh yes." This time, her smile was radiant.

"Isn't it safe to assume with time we might explore other things you might like? If we take it slow, and if we don't take you by surprise?"

He watched as the light faded from her eyes, and she shifted away from him.

"You don't understand."

"Then help me too." Damn, they'd been so close. Even now the faint scent of her arousal teased his senses.

"I can't. It just won't work." She pushed against his chest, and he let her go. "It's not you, it's me." *Were there any words a man hated more?*

"I'm tired, Jack. I want to go to bed."

He watched as she made her way down the hall to the bedroom. He winced as she shut the door behind her.

****

Four days later the US Marshals brought Mr. and Mrs. Hidalgo to Southern California in the middle of the night. They would be staying in a hotel in Orange County, halfway between San Diego and Santa Monica. It was decided the best place for the family to meet would be the bungalow in Santa Monica.

Jack still wasn't happy the US Marshals knew Beth's whereabouts, but he'd been assured only a select few knew, and they'd been vetted by the leadership within their organization.

Jack watched as the older couple came into the house. The girls were the spitting image of their mother. Gloria Hildalgo was overwhelmed at seeing her daughters. But Jack stood in back of Lydia and Beth, both literally and figuratively watching Mr. Hildalgo. He knew he was their father, but his actions had gotten them targeted for execution. Yep, he had Beth's back, and since Clint wasn't here, he had Lydia's too.

"My babies!" Mrs. Hidalgo ran to her girls with tears streaming down her face.

Both women rushed towards her, their arms open, and all three enveloped one another in one big hug. Rapid-fire Spanish made it so Jack could barely keep up.

Mr. Hidalgo stared at the group, and then looked at him. They assessed one another. He knew Jack was judging him, nodded, slowly walked towards his little family, and wrapped his arms around the three women. He said nothing, just rested his chin on his wife's head. It would have been a touching scene if Jack could have gotten past the vision in his head of Beth being attacked by the men in the jungle.

131

Beth had dinner all prepped in the kitchen. Finally, Jack made a move towards the open kitchen and was immediately swarmed by the three Hidalgo women, led by Gloria.

"Absolutely not, no man is allowed in the kitchen when I am here." She bustled past Jack, and Lydia followed with Beth in the rear. Beth shrugged her shoulders and rolled her eyes as if to say, 'what can I do'? Jack headed back towards the living room where Ricardo Hidalgo stood hunched over with a defiant look in his eyes.

"I don't think we were properly introduced. I am Ricardo Hidalgo, and I believe you are Jack Preston, a Navy SEAL, yes?"

"Yes, Sir." Jack shook the man's proffered hand.

"It is also my understanding you are responsible for saving my daughter's life. I owe you a debt as I owe many of your compatriots."

"You owe me nothing." Jack didn't want any debts owed either way between the two of them.

"Fine. There will be no more talk of this. But you seem to be very protective of my daughters. This I do not understand. You will explain yourself," he demanded arrogantly. The man was no longer hunched over. *Very interesting*.

"Why should I explain anything to you?"

"I have made mistakes. Grave mistakes. I have had much time to consider them. I will be here to make amends with my daughters if they allow it. It will be between them and me. However, I will do everything in my power to protect them going forward. This includes ensuring they come to no further harm."

"Let me get this straight. You acknowledge I saved your daughter's life, and now you're saying I'm going to harm her?"

"It is my right. I am her father. I am the head of this household."

"Yes, you are her father."

"*I* am the one who will care for her, and ensure her safety."

Jack stifled a laugh, and Hidalgo's face flushed dark with anger.

"Do not take me lightly, boy."

For long moments, Jack considered the man. His Southern upbringing came into play—this was his elder, and father of the woman he loved. As such he was due respect. As a matter of fact, he was asserting his rights to protect his daughters, so he should be applauded. But all Jack wanted to do was throat punch the bastard.

133

Looking over his shoulder, he saw Gloria and Lydia were busy talking and laughing, but Beth was watching them.

"Sounds wonderful, Ricardo," Jack said loudly enough for Beth to hear. After she had turned back to her mother and sister, his gaze slid to Hidalgo.

"Listen here old man, you work really hard to make amends with your daughters. They deserve to have a father who licks their shoes for the rest of their lives after what you did. But don't think you can threaten me, or for that matter Clint, ever again. We're the men who are going to protect Lydia and Beth from now on. We're responsible for their safety, and we'll never put them in harm's way like you did. If you do one more Goddamn thing to cause them one more tear in this life, you'll answer to us. I suggest *you* don't take *me*, lightly."

"Jack, how's it going in here? Are you and Papa about ready for dinner?" Beth asked as she came into the living room.

"We're having a great time, aren't we, Ricardo?"

"Yes. Yes, we are." The man was once again hunched over as he gave his daughter a kiss on the cheek.

****

"I'm going to the hotel with your parents and the Marshals. I want to talk to them about their security," Jack said.

Beth and Lydia looked at each other, perplexed at first. "He wants to make sure they don't have any fucking leaks like they did with me," Lydia said after she realized his intentions. Jack had already left, but Beth watched through the front room window as he got into the SUV. Lydia was probably right. Their watchdogs were still in place, too.

"He's pretty damn protective of you," Lydia said as they plopped down on the couch.

"Like Clint isn't the same way," Beth countered. "Have I told you how happy I am for you? Clint is so wonderful. I loved the way he took care of you in the jungle. You've deserved wonderful for forever."

"He is, isn't he?" She shook her head in amazement. "He wants to marry me."

Beth closed her eyes and gave thanks. She took her sister's hands in hers. "I hope you said yes. If you didn't, I'll cut off your hair in your sleep."

They laughed, remembering when Beth had tried to do it with her dull childhood scissors when she was four.

"He hasn't officially asked me. But yes, I said yes." Beth's relief was palpable.

"What about you? Your big blonde god is amazing. Jack certainly looks like he adores you. But even better, you allowed him to touch you."

Beth's face heated, she looked away, and then turned back. "I need to talk to you. I'm so confused."

"What, baby girl?"

"He's talked about a future with me."

Lydia tucked a strand of hair behind Beth's ear. "That's wonderful. You two seem great together. Am I missing something?"

"He's too good."

"That's not possible. Nobody is too good for my sister."

"You're biased." Beth forced a weak laugh. "Anyway, I keep freezing up on him. He thinks I'll get past it, but I know I never will." Lydia stroked her arm.

"Okay, can you tell me about it?"

"I haven't been completely honest. Something happened before the cabin. I was scared of men before then. The cabin solidified it."

Lydia stared at her for a moment with dawning comprehension.

"Oh baby, why didn't you tell someone? Our parents? Me?"

"I couldn't."

"Yes, you could." Lydia grabbed her hands and pulled her closer. "Tell me now."

"It happened one of those times at Papa's office."

"Oh fuck. I think I know where this is going." Lydia looked scared and mad.

"What?"

"Tell me."

"I was a sophomore. Remember when I used to help with the filing?" Beth's thoughts hyper-focused to one of the moments in her father's office.

"Papa's office was such a place of pleasure. The files gleamed brightly and it was my responsibility to make sure everything was in order. I used my best printing to make sure every tab was readable, and everything was color coded so Papa could find them easily."

The files were kept in a little room down the hall from Papa's main office and three times a week it was my kingdom. I was in there filing when the door opened, I turned to smile at Papa, but it wasn't him.

"Oh, hello. I think you're lost. Papa's office is two doors down." She smiled respectfully. She'd met

137

Alberto Guzman twice before, and she knew he and his father were important clients.

"I know. He's busy with my father. I thought I'd find you."

He walked into the room, and she realized her domain was very small. He continued forward and her hip hit the open file cabinet drawer.

"Mr. Guzman, is there something I can help you with?" Her voice sounded scared even to her own ears. She had to be misunderstanding the situation.

"I've been watching you for months. You're beautiful, Elsbeth." She lost her voice. She took another step backward, and her heel hit the bottom of the file cabinet. She winced. Mr. Guzman stroked his hand down her cheek to her chest until it rested above her breast.

"I'm going to kiss you. Have you ever been kissed before?" She shook her head, hair flying wildly. He gave a raspy laugh, and used both hands to push it out of her face, his palms were clammy. His breath was hot as he came closer.

Then his mouth was on hers. She imagined his lips were what two worms would feel like, and his tongue, as it forced itself inside her mouth, was like a slug. She pushed against him, but it was no use he was too strong. She gagged.

One hand wrapped around her back, forcing her tight against him, she couldn't move. Then she felt his other hand clawing under the skirt of her school uniform. Ahh God, she felt fingers crawling under her cotton panties. She tried to scream, but she couldn't. No air. She was going to die.

Pain, red hot pain, as he shoved into her.

"Berto! We have to go. Where are you?"

He released her, and she fell in a heap on the floor. Her arm slammed against the corner of the file cabinet, and tears and snot covered her face.

"Look at me, Elsbeth." She did, scared not to.

"Even crying, you're beautiful. I'll be back for you."

"Berto!"

"Remember, we own your father if you say anything, well, let's just say bad things would happen. Do you understand?"

She just stared up at a monster.

"Elsbeth! Tell me you understand."

She nodded, trying to focus despite the pain radiating between her legs.

"Say the words."

The door pushed open. "Come on, Berto, we have to go." Alfonso Guzman ignored her.

"Elsbeth, don't you have something to say?"

"I'll tell no one."

"Very good." He turned to his father. "I'm ready. We have reservations, don't we?" The door closed behind the two men.

"Beth, honey. Can you hear me?"

"Lydia?" It sounded like she was far away. Beth shook her head to clear it.

"Oh thank God, you're back with me." Beth looked at her sister. She was crying. Then she realized she'd actually said all of it out loud.

"Ahhh, Lydia, I never meant to tell you." Lydia grasped her shoulders and pulled her close. She was shaking.

"Oh baby girl. I'm sorry, so sorry."

She pulled the afghan from the back of the couch and wrapped it around Beth's shoulders.

"I don't understand. Why didn't you tell Mama or Papa?" Lydia seemed to shimmer in front of her. She shook her head.

"Tell me. I want to understand."

"You were off at University. I spent so much time at the office with Papa. The Guzman's work was almost all of his business," Beth whispered. "He wouldn't have a business without them."

"It wouldn't have mattered. You know that. You *have* to have known that."

Beth clutched the blanket tighter trying to control the shivers. She remembered back to that time. Remembered pushing herself up off the floor, and somehow making it to the little restroom. She'd cleaned up and gone back to filing. She'd hidden it away in a box and most times it never entered her consciousness. But still it had loomed large. She'd changed everything about her life. School had scared her. She could only handle small gatherings. She took stairs instead of elevators to avoid closed in spaces with men. From that day forward she'd lived a different life.

"It wasn't important, I managed."

"Dammit. I should've seen this. There were signs. There were so many things going on in this family I should've seen if I wasn't so focused on my own goals." Lydia sounded furious. Beth reached out to pat her hand.

"Lydia, it's okay."

141

"Oh honey, I don't need your reassurance." Lydia saw Beth's hand was trembling. "Hold on a second, I want to get you something warm to drink."

"I'm not thirsty."

"You need to keep your strength up, and I want to talk to you about something else. We're going to finally clear the air once and for all."

Beth had no idea what she was talking about, but she sat there while Lydia went in the kitchen. Beth heard her rustling around but she wasn't really paying much attention. She was glad her father was finally trying his best to bring the monster's father to justice. Hopefully, when he testified in the next few days, they'd find evidence against Berto and he'd go to prison.

"Here honey, drink this."

Lydia wrapped Beth's hands around a warm mug. Inhaling the scent of chocolate and cinnamon made Beth smile.

"You used Mama's recipe."

"Of course."

Beth sipped her cocoa and rested against Lydia as she sat beside her on the sofa. They sat that way until she finished her drink.

"Did you ever tell your counselor about this?"

"Hmm? No, we just talked about the cabin."

"You were letting Jack touch you again today. I've seen him with his arm around you. Has he kissed you?" Beth's cheeks heated and it wasn't from the hot chocolate.

"Why are you asking me?"

"Because all things considered it's a fucking miracle. Now answer the question. Have you let the man kiss you?"

"Yes."

Lydia plucked the mug out of her hands, put it on the floor, and flung her arms around Beth crying out with joy. Beth hugged her back. It felt so good for someone else to finally know everything.

"Tell me about him."

"He's wonderful. He's so patient and so kind. He seems to know what I need even when I don't know. I feel safe with him."

"He's damn good to look at too."

"I hadn't noticed," Beth said primly and both women laughed. When they finally caught their breath, Lydia continued her questioning.

"How far have these kisses gone?"

143

"I freeze. It's so unfair to him. I've told him we have to stop. As soon as this whole mess is over with I'm going to insist he leave me alone. He needs a *real* woman. A *whole* woman."

Lydia sucked in her breath. "What did he say to that?"

"No."

"You need to tell me what he said," Lydia insisted, misunderstanding Beth.

"That's what he said, 'no.' He said he's not letting me go."

"I knew I liked him, now I think I love him."

"Be serious."

"I am serious. If you can kiss him, you can do more. Your body is responding, and he's patient. But you need, to be honest with him. He needs to know everything he's up against."

Beth closed her eyes and took a deep breath. "It's not that easy. I'm scared. Every time he tries to touch my breasts I flash back to the room. If he were to ever try anything more...I know it's going to hurt. I never flash back to the cabin because it's not the same thing. I don't know why."

"It could be any number of reasons. You talked about the cabin with Nancy. It was a totally different situation—not nearly as intimate. You weren't so young. It was your first time with a man."

"Enough already."

"I'm just saying, who the hell knows why you react that way. Bottom line, do you know it won't hurt?"

Beth turned away from Lydia's gaze.

"Shit."

"I know logically what happens. It's just I don't think it will happen for me. I don't think my body is capable of becoming aroused. So I think it's always going to hurt."

"So tell Jack. Let him know you have that concern. He'll back off if it's hurting you. It's different with each man. I've been more aroused with some than others. If Jack is anything like Clint, he'll know what to do, and he'll make sure you feel pleasure."

"But I don't want to tease him."

"You need to talk to him first."

Beth took a deep breath. It's the first time she really had hope. She was pretty sure she loved this man. Beth wanted a chance to make this work, so she'd take her sister's advice.

Chapter Eleven

Jack thought he might throw up.

Guzman was going to die! Done deal.

But the most important thing was Beth.

"Now can I hold you?" Beth trembled so hard, he thought she might fly apart. She'd insisted on sitting a cushion away from him on the couch, and he'd respected her request. As she told more of her story, it slowly killed him. He'd never seen her so pale, not even in the hospital.

"I don't know. Do you want to?"

"Fuck yeah, I want to." He knew his face didn't show his real emotions, that he looked calm and supportive. It was a countenance he'd perfected dealing with his mom when they were living in the women's shelter.

"Come on over here, would you, girl?" It was important she make the first move. She flung herself at him. Gripping him tight around the waist, and she was making little mewling noises.

"I've got you." He stroked her hair and laid kisses wherever he could reach. She rocked side to side, and he rocked with her. Finally, he picked her up and put her on his lap. She cuddled but still didn't lift her face from his chest. The mewling stopped, though, and he took that as a good thing.

Beth coughed.

"Sweetheart, do you want some water?" She nodded into his chest. Extricating himself, he took the moment to look at her face, and then he kissed the tip of her nose. "Be right back."

He took the time in the kitchen to take a few deep breaths. Pictures of a young Beth lying in a heap in some dusty little room kept flashing in front of him. He pushed his balled up hands into his eyes, trying to relieve the pressure and get rid of the images. It didn't work. He got Beth her glass of water and went back to the sofa in the living room.

Crouched in front of her, he flashed back to the first time he met her in the Dallas hospital. "Drink this." She finished it, and he set it on the coffee table. He picked her up and settled her on his lap again.

"I'm sorry that happened to you, Beth. No child deserves to have their innocence taken away."

She snorted. "Your mom told me about your dad. You went through much worse. I wasn't even raped."

He tilted her chin so she was forced to look him in the eye.

"This isn't some kind of contest. And no, this isn't even in the same ballpark. You were too raped. We're not going to get technical but he raped you sweetheart, and what's worse, he raped your soul." Tears welled, and two fell from her eyes.

"Jack, I don't know what to do. I feel so broken inside. You keep saying you're not letting me go, but now you have to see there isn't any hope."

For the first time since she started talking, Jack gave her a *real* smile.

"You've got it wrong. Now there *is* hope. Now I *know* we're going to make it. It amazes me how responsive you've been so far, but now that you've told me and Lydia you can finally move forward. Sure it might take some time, but sweetheart, you're the furthest thing from broken there is."

She stared into the distance, and eventually looked at him with a tentative smile. "It doesn't feel as heavy in my heart anymore."

"That's what happens when you share a burden, it lightens."

"It has."

"I'm glad. Because I want you to listen to me and really hear me." He waited for her to look at him, her black eyes warmed and she nodded.

"I'm listening. You can tell me anything, Jack."

"Good, because I don't think you've been ready for me to say this before." He cupped the side of her face and traced her bottom lip with his thumb. "I love you, Beth. Not the love and admiration of a friend kind of love. The kind of love where I see us on a front porch when we're ninety with great grandkids running around. I'll still want to hold you in my arms as we drift asleep each night. That kind of love."

He watched her struggle and felt a monumental sense of relief when she didn't immediately say she couldn't be what he needed.

Her fingers gripped her opal pendant, and she bit her lip.

"Sweetheart. Talk to me."

"I still have trouble seeing past my own shadows, so the future is tough for me, okay?"

He nodded. It made sense

"But you Jack Preston...you, I see just fine. You fill my vision and light my way. I love you so much, and it's not because I need you, or depend on you. It's because you're such a loving, strong, and caring man. I might not be able to see the front porch scene yet,

150

but I want it. I love you too. I love you. I love you. I love you."

"Halleluiah!" He hugged her tight, she started to laugh, and so did he. Tonight was the night they officially made love. They might not have physically come together, but their souls had finally joined. Much later, she drifted off to sleep in his arms, and Jack stood up to take her to the bedroom.

"What?" Beth asked groggily.

"Sleep, sweetheart, I have you." He walked down the hall and opened the door to her bedroom. Checking to make sure everything seemed in order, he placed Beth in the middle of the bed. When he went to stand up, Beth grabbed his shirt.

"Don't leave," she said softly.

"I'm not going anywhere you don't want me to go." Jack stared down at Beth, she looked like a rumpled angel. "Let me get you out of these shoes and under the covers."

"You'll stay with me, won't you?"

"Wild horses couldn't drag me away."

After he got her situated under the covers, he stretched out on top of the duvet and tucked her close to his side.

"Thank you, Jack, I don't think I could have gone back to sleep without you here with me."

"Well, that's good news because I couldn't have rested tonight if you weren't in my arms." She kissed the bottom of his chin and was soon breathing deeply.

****

The next morning the Hidalgo family intended to get together one more time before the trial the following day, but Beth was still asleep at ten in the morning when Lydia called.

"She's still asleep, yesterday was hard on her. She needs to stay in and rest today."

"Did she talk to you?" Lydia asked tentatively.

"Yes, she did. Thank you for telling her she needed to speak to me." Jack paused, it took him a moment to clear his throat and come up with the right words. "I think it helped her. God, I hope it did."

"How..." Lydia paused. "How are you doing? I mean how did you react?"

"How did I react? I'm pissed as fuck! Somebody is going to die. But for her sake I didn't show it. All that's important is she feel loved and safe, so I stayed calm."

"Exactly right. You're doing it exactly right, Jack."

"Stupid isn't part of the recruiting criteria for SEALs, Lydia. I thought you knew that by now."

She laughed. "Just take care of my baby sister. I'll take care of my parents. I'll also make sure my papa still has, at least, some of his manly parts attached."

"What do you mean by that?"

"I just mean you shouldn't think Beth or I are stupid either. Goodbye."

Jack grinned as he hung up the phone, and then he went to the living room window to see who was on duty. He waved to Terry and Chris, who had taken over for Lou and Mike. After making another pot of coffee, he checked on Beth. Half the time during the night when she was so restless, he'd thought it was because she was still dressed, but he didn't want to wake her up so she could get into her sleep shirt. She was still in her clothes from the day before with the covers bunched around her waist. At least now she seemed to be really sleeping. He went into the other room and closed the door behind him.

Grabbing his phone he called a familiar number. "Hi Jack, how's California?"

"It's bad and it's good, Mom." Jack's voice broke. He looked down the hall and realized he couldn't trust the door wouldn't open.

"Are you all right? Is Beth?"

"We're fine now. Hold on." He went to the laundry room and shut the door. He rested his back against it before continuing to talk. "I'm back."

"Can you talk now? Tell me." And he did. It rushed out of him like a breaking wave. Jack didn't know everything he said, or what words he used. Every time he stopped his Mom would gently prod him along. He heard her tears and realized his face was wet.

"She didn't deserve this Mom. I know this happens. I know you suffered so much. But she didn't deserve this."

"Nobody does."

"What can I do to help her?"

"You listen to her, and you love her. It's the two things you're already doing, son."

"It doesn't seem like enough."

"It is. Trust me, it is. It also sounds like I might have a daughter-in-law soon."

"Damn straight." Jack grinned, and then he heard a sound coming from the kitchen.

"I've got to go."

"I love you. You give my love to Beth."

He hung up the phone. He opened the door and found Beth opening the dishwasher. "What do you need?"

"I'm getting a bowl for some cereal." She was freshly showered.

"What kind?" he asked, opening the pantry door. She didn't answer him, and when he turned around, she was blushing.

"Froot Loops it is." He laughed. Grabbing the box from the pantry, he put it on the table and got the milk from the refrigerator. He snagged a bowl and spoon for himself and sat down at the table with her.

"When did you become a fan of Toucan Sam?" Jack asked, indicating the colorful bird on the outside of the box.

"Since forever. And don't try to take the prize from the cereal box, Preston, it's all mine," Beth said as she poured her milk into the cereal bowl.

"You think you can really take it from me?"

"I fight dirty. Lydia never won the prize, and she was older. The prize always goes to me." She smirked. Beth took her first bite of cereal and a smile suffused her face. "This is bliss." Jack ate a spoonful. It wasn't bliss, but seeing Beth act so carefree after all of the horrors of yesterday was a gift from Heaven.

"Your family left to visit the beach. They said they'd call you when they're done."

"Lydia didn't tell Mama and Papa about Berto, did she?" Beth's spoon clattered into her bowl, spilling milk and cereal everywhere.

"Oh sweetheart, I can't imagine she would tell anyone without your permission." He got up to get some paper towels. Squatting beside her, he cleaned up the mess.

"Are you sure?" It was quite telling Beth didn't want her parents to know about it. They were the two people she should have relied on through the harrowing experience.

Jack threw the soiled paper in the trash, then came back and hugged Beth. "I'm absolutely positive. She would never betray your trust." She relaxed into his hold, her breath sighing against his neck.

"I really should be with them. Papa testifies tomorrow. This is the last day for us to spend as a family before his ordeal." Jack couldn't give a shit less.

"Sweetheart, Lydia has it covered. Anyway, I have a surprise for you today."

"Really? What?"

"First you have to get all of your daily vitamins and nutrients from the mega-dose of sugar known as

Froot Loops and I'll tell you." He grinned, as he got her a new bowl and spoon.

He sat back across from her and dived into the cereal with relish, matching her spoonful to spoonful. Okay, he had to admit, he had Fruity Pebbles at his condo. Who didn't like morning crack sometimes? As soon as her last bite was eaten she rested her spoon in the empty bowl and looked at him expectantly.

"Tell me my surprise."

"Better yet, I'll show you. Go and put on your oldest pair of jeans and I'll give you one of my T-Shirts to wear."

"So this is a fancy date," she said as she rushed down the hall brimming with excitement. He pulled a clean T-Shirt out of his duffle and knocked on her door.

"Come in." He hesitated. Seeing her in any sort of undress was going to kill him. She turned around, and he saw her in a tank top with hip hugger jeans. Yep, death by Beth.

"I brought the T-Shirt."

"Tell me my surprise, and I'll give you the plastic spoon I got out of the box of Froot Loops," she coaxed. Jack watched transfixed as she pulled on the T-Shirt. Beth had a great body, and his body approved. *Damn, keep it together Preston.*

157

"If it was the blue spoon, I would've told you, but since you fished out the pink spoon, you'll just have to wait. Let's head to the car."

Jack already called Mrs. Marsh, and by the time they got to the little co-op garden in San Diego, she was waiting for them.

"Jack!" she called out. "I'm over here."

"What is this place?" Beth asked as they walked down the paths towards the senior citizen.

"This is a shared garden. For those of us who live in apartments and condos, and don't have yards, we can garden and grow food in a collective piece of land. I thought you might enjoy working in Mrs. Marsh's garden with her. You'll love her. She's the one who keeps my plants alive whenever I'm overseas."

"Jack, who is this beautiful girl you've brought today? Is she your girlfriend?"

"Yes, she is. I done good, didn't I Mrs. M?"

"Well if she can use gardening tools, then I'll approve. I'm Sarah Marsh, what's your name?"

"I'm Beth." Jack knew it was easier at this point for her to stick with a first name than try to remember the new last name she'd been given.

"Well Beth, do you know the difference between weeds, and actual cabbage, carrots, and beans?"

"I do."

"Excellent! I have an extra set of knee pads and gloves. Let's get you started." After Mrs. Marsh got Beth situated, she turned to Jack.

"You know what you need to do."

"Yes, Ma'am." He grinned. He went to the parking lot and helped all the different people—mostly strangers—unload their cars, and bring their supplies into the fenced in garden. Mrs. Marsh told him early on when he'd come to work in her garden that first he had to put his back to work helping all the tired old people. She'd winked when she'd said it. But when he saw all the loads people carried, he definitely saw her point.

By the time he got back to work Mrs. Marsh's row of tomatoes, he saw they were fast friends and Beth was back to her old self. He'd hit a home run.

One of the other women from the co-op came over to Beth and started speaking in Spanish. Soon they were involved in an intense conversation about different types of peppers for cooking.

"Even though you haven't asked, yes, all of your plants are doing fine. Now tell me about Beth, she's lovely."

"She is isn't she?"

"Inside and out. I'd always hoped you were smart enough to look for substance as well as flash. I see you were." He looked at Mrs. Marsh and smiled.

"We're going to have to be going soon. I needed to give her some time to wind down. I appreciate you meeting us out here."

"It wasn't a problem at all." The older woman smiled. Beth came over.

"I think it's about time I got you some lunch. We can go by my place and get cleaned up first. Mrs. Marsh, would you like to come with us?"

"I have a date, honey. You two run along. Beth, thanks for all of your help. Jack, thanks for only pulling up two of my tomato plants this time."

"Hey wait a minute."

"I'm teasing, I'm teasing." Beth and Mrs. Marsh exchanged a significant glance and Jack sighed. He'd really tried, but he probably pulled up two of her tomato plants.

****

Jack amazed her. He seemed to always find the right things for her to do. But wasn't it getting old? Everything being about her? They got back to Santa Monica at four o'clock. She'd gotten a call from her sister letting her know they were all going to have dinner near the water, and what time to join them.

"Lydia, I think I'm going to bow out tonight." There was a long pause on the phone. Beth could practically hear her sister's mental gears turning.

"You want some time alone with Jack. I get it."

"I'll call you tomorrow. You three have fun."

"Call me if you need anything. I do mean *anything*."

"I won't. I'm covered." Beth hung up the phone.

Jack closed the blinds after watching the trade-off of shifts between Mike, Lou, Chris, and Terry.

"We're not going out with Lydia and your folks?"

"Nope, we're going to do what you want to do tonight. Watch sports, a movie, go to a bar. Something you would do if I wasn't around." He looked at her like she'd grown a second head.

"Going out with you and your family sounded nice."

"I'm sick of everything revolving around me. You haven't done one thing that's made you happy since we've met. It's been all about Beth Hidalgo and her needs."

"Uhhhm. Where is this coming from?"

"Even today, you took me to the garden so I could relax after yesterday. Once again putting me first. Well, now we put you first." He stalked across the

161

room, and suddenly she had a big blonde man towering over her.

"Are you out of your mind? Where is this coming from?"

"It's true. Everything is about me. I want something to be about you."

"Think this through. The reason I knew to take you to the co-op garden is because I go there sometimes with Mrs. Marsh. When we were on the ranch, I took you horseback riding because I like to ride horses. We sat around and read books because that's something I like to do." He looked totally frustrated.

"But still, since knowing me, you've been glued to my hip. You haven't had any alone time. You haven't had a chance to go out with any of your friends."

"My friends are my teammates. Most of them have been either on maneuvers or deployed. When all of this is over with, yes, I want you to meet them. I want you to spend time getting to know them. They are a great bunch of guys. What about you? Your life's been on hold."

She looked at him with dawning comprehension. Her life had been on hold for seven years. Ever since the moment in the file room, her life had been on hold. Before then she'd wanted so much more. It wasn't just that she wanted to be a wife and mother. She wanted to work with children too. Really work with them on a professional level.

Beth thought about what she left behind in Mexico and it really wasn't all that much. Except for her time volunteering at the school she was damn near a shut-in. All of her drive and ambition had stopped in one dusty room in fifteen horrifying minutes.

"I used to want to be a teacher."

"I wondered why you hadn't pursued college like Lydia."

"I think I've been in stasis."

"That makes total sense."

"It's stupid," she said bitterly. All those wasted years.

"What are you thinking?"

"I'm disgusted with myself. I look at all Lydia has accomplished, and it seems all I've done is cooked and cleaned."

"The way Lydia tells it; you've made a hell of a difference to those children in the community center." That brought her up short.

"Jack, it's the other way around. They saved me. Those kids are so special and so loving. I don't think I could have kept it together if it weren't for them." He folded her in his arms, and she breathed him in. His cheek lightly rested on the top of her head.

163

"When it's done right, it's what happens in a relationship. You end up saving one another." She stood for long moments, her arms wrapped around the warm, gentle giant.

"I still want us to do a Jack thing. Movie? Sports? Football—your American kind?"

"It's not football season, otherwise yes. But sure let's see what's on Netflix. I vote for showers first." Beth jumped back.

"Oh, I must stink!"

"Not even on your ripest day do I think you could stink." Jack smiled. She grimaced and headed towards the bedroom to get a change of clothes for after her shower.

As she smoothed the vanilla scented soap over her body, Beth noticed something. She liked the feel of her skin under her hands. She'd never really thought about it before, bathing had always been a chore. Actually, sometimes her body made her uncomfortable, a little unclean, like something needed to be washed a little more vigorously. Not today, today it felt like her skin needed to be pampered with the foamy suds.

She got out of the shower and slathered on the matching vanilla lotion. She hardly ever put lotion on her skin, but today she thought of Jack noticing the softness and the scent and she shivered. She caught sight of herself in the mirror. Her cheeks were flushed, and her hair was full and wavy. She almost looked pretty.

Maybe she'd been in stasis in *all* aspects of her life because of what the bastard had done to her. Well, he wasn't going to win anymore. This was *her* life. She was going to take it back, dammit.

Beth got dressed and went into the living room. Jack still wasn't there. She rummaged around until she found some caramel corn, and put it into the microwave. Her fingers trembled as she punched in the numbers.

"It's just Jack," she murmured to herself.

"What about me?" he said from behind her. She whirled around.

"I was thinking about you." She blushed.

"I got that." He had a killer grin.

"Look, you...you..."

"Smart-ass, the term you're looking for is smart-ass."

The buzzer rang, and as she was about to grab the bag of popcorn he stopped her.

"It's hot baby, let me." He pulled out the bag by the corner and put it on the counter.

"So why were you talking about me?"

"I was telling myself why it would be okay if we tried to do more than just kiss. I was reminding myself it was you." She enjoyed the way he froze in place. It served the smart-ass right.

"How much more?" he asked hoarsely. "I mean, only as much as you're comfortable with, of course."

Beth grasped one of his hands and nuzzled her cheek against his palm. With the other, she touched the dark blonde stubble on his face and traced his dimple. His eyes were solemn as they looked down at her.

She slipped her hand around the back of his neck and tugged slightly, loving the way his eyes warmed, and he bent towards her. She'd ached to kiss him again, and prayed she could handle more this time.

"No expectations, sweetheart. I'll be happy with a kiss." Once again he'd read her mind. Beth melted against him, and he picked her up as if she weighed nothing. It was like something out of a girlish dream and she reveled in it.

He sat on the couch and nestled her in his lap. She'd kept her arm around his neck, and then stroked it into his hair. It had gotten a little longer since their stay on the ranch, and felt like warm silk.

"For the moment, just a kiss. I *need* a kiss. Your kiss." He tilted her chin and brushed her lower lip down with his thumb. She swiped her tongue against it, and he groaned.

"You're going to burn me up before we even get started." He feathered a gentle kiss on her temple, gliding ever closer to her lips. She held her breath in anticipation until he finally rested his lips on the side of her mouth. She turned her head and captured his mouth.

He groaned, and soon his tongue was curled around hers, and she heard a whimper rise from her that wasn't fear, it was need. Jack must have realized because he pressed closer. His fingers tangled in her hair as his hand coaxed her closer, slanting her so their mouths met at the perfect angle. Their noses brushed, just another caress, another connection making Beth melt into the moment with this man.

Her blood heated, and she squirmed on his lap. When she felt his need, she paused and Jack broke the kiss.

"No, don't stop."

"Sweetheart, I told you 'just a kiss.'"

"I want to make a goal." He looked perplexed, and then laughed out loud.

"You mean you want to go to second base?"

Now *she* didn't know what *he* was talking about, but one way or another she needed his hands on her breasts. She unbuttoned the top two buttons of her blouse. He stayed her hand.

"Beth, are you sure?" Her fingers touched the opal necklace at her throat, and she smiled.

"I'm positive."

"Then let me."

His knuckles brushed her skin as he unbuttoned the rest of her blouse, his hands slipped the cotton off her shoulders and he trailed kisses on her collarbone. She reached to unfasten the front clasp of her bra, but again, he stopped her.

"Please, Beth, this is my fantasy." It wasn't possible, but when she looked at him, he gave a solemn nod. "I love you, Beth, I've dreamed of seeing you, touching you, pleasing you." She blinked fast, fighting back tears.

Then his hands cupped her bare breasts and thought was beyond her. There was only sensation.

"Ahhh." He softly molded her flesh, and she watched. His strong hands holding her tender flesh was mesmerizing. When his thumbs brushed her nipples she arched up, her gaze flashing to his face, needing reassurance as every cell in her body lit up.

"Too much?"

"I'm not sure." He stopped. "No, don't stop. I like it. A lot." She put her hands over his and looked down.

She gave a choked laugh. They were so small in comparison.

His lips pressed against the side of her neck and her laugh changed to a sigh. "More please." This time, he laughed.

"So polite." He lightly suckled her throat and his thumbs rasped. Beth's eyes drifted closed as she started to float.

"Beth? Beth, are you with me?" She jerked at the feel of his teeth on her neck, and she moaned as he scraped them downwards to her shoulder.

"Do I have your attention?"

"Yes, Jack." It was a puff of air.

"Any fear?"

She searched, and if she was honest, his erection did scare her. But then again it didn't because it was Jack, and he would never force her. But then it did because she would never be able to please him. It was all mixed up in her head. His teeth nipped her again.

"Beth, stay with me. Remember, you're in charge. We're only making as many goals as you want to."

"Bases. We're making bases," she corrected him.

169

His tongue laved over where he'd bitten and she shivered.

He moved his hands and brought his head down. She cried out as his tongue touched her nipple. So warm and soft, her head swirled with delight as she realized this was yet another form of loving.

****

Beth caught fire in his arms. Jack hadn't expected she would burn so bright and so fast. He looked up at her face and saw her biting her lip her face suffused with passion. He was scared, but it had never stopped him before, and it wasn't going to stop him now. This was the most important mission of his life.

Her brow furrowed as she began to rock back and forth in his lap. It was clear to him what she needed. He continued to taste the sublime texture of her nipple, licking, savoring, and then he took the brown rose nub into his mouth. She arched into him with a sigh. He continued to hold her breast to his lips while his other hand began a languid journey down her torso.

He knew Beth was unaware of her rocking, the way her legs had shifted and were now slightly spread apart. Her soft buttocks tortured his erection, and her legs attempted to clamp around his knee. He stroked further downwards, easing over the waistband of her Capri pants. She jerked.

Her hands were suddenly there, and he couldn't help a second of disappointment he immediately tamped down. But her hands slid underneath his, and she was unbuttoning her trousers and lowering the zipper.

He considered, and knew he needed to take this opportunity to show her she could. She made a frustrated sound as the zipper caught.

"Shhhh, I've got it. They train us in complicated machinery." She gave a little giggle. Just what he wanted. Her hands stayed on her zipper, as if not sure where to go.

"I love it when you touch my hair," he coaxed.

"You do?" He looked at her and smiled. "Don't you like it when I touch yours?"

"Yes." She reached up to put and her arms around his neck, her hands playing in his hair.

He kissed her, once again luxuriating in the taste of Beth Hidalgo.

She relaxed, and he unzipped her pants, easing his hand inside the front of her silky panties. Her curls were damp. He dipped down further, nudging her tender folds apart, finding her drenched. He brought some of that moisture upwards and began to gently circle her engorged bud.

171

She broke off the kiss, and buried her head in the crook of his neck, panting. He continued his ministrations. She pushed against him, hard. Understanding her wordless command, he increased his speed and pressure.

She sobbed into his neck. "I can't."

"You can. You were meant to fly in my arms."

"I can't, it won't work."

Jack heard the frustration in her voice, how she was working herself into a self-fulfilling prophecy. With his free hand, he tilted her head up and gave her a reassuring smile. He kissed her, plunging his tongue into her mouth. She sucked him inside. At the same moment, he slid one finger inside her sheath. Her head arched backward, the tendons in her neck rigid, and she let loose a silent scream.

****

He'd done it. She'd done it. She was shaking. Beth collapsed into the arms of the man she loved, shuddering in ecstasy. She felt his erection and wasn't scared, she saw nothing but patience, satisfaction, and love in his eyes.

"Beth."

"What?"

"Just Beth. Always and forever, it will be just Beth."

Chapter Twelve

Jack looked at the beautiful woman lying on the bed and slid in beside her. He'd gotten up early, even though all he wanted to do was stay with her curled up beside him.

Last night after their gentle love making he coaxed her towards the bedroom. She hesitantly tried to disrobe in front of him, but he'd said he was changing in the guest bath, and saw her relief.

"But you're going to sleep with me, right?" she asked anxiously.

"Wild horses couldn't keep me out of your bed tonight." She relaxed and smiled.

When he got back to the bedroom, she was under the covers, and fairly vibrating with tension. He decided to take the Band-Aid approach and slipped in under the sheets beside her. She was cold.

"Come here sweetheart, let me warm you up."

"I don't know why I'm so nervous, you've held me in bed before."

"This is different, and we both know it."

She looked at him with big solemn black eyes and nodded.

"But it's different in a good way." She moved closer to him and sighed. "You're warm."

"That's what happens when you're so big, you exude body heat."

"I like it with your shirt off." She ran her hands over his chest, and he thought he might spontaneously combust.

He inched closer until they were pressed together, and her head rested on his chest. Jack noticed she had her thigh against his erection and it didn't seem to bother her, but it sure as hell bothered him. There was no doubt in his mind he wouldn't be getting any sleep, and he'd been right. But he'd come up with a plan.

The sun was up and she looked beautiful in the morning light.

"You're staring at me again."

"I'd be a fool not to." He leaned in for a kiss. She melted like powder sugar against his lips. Before things could go too far, he pulled back.

"Up. We're getting up."

"Why? I like it right here. I want to make some more goals."

Jack gave a strained laugh and lifted her hand off his chest.

"Off you go. Into the shower with you. We're going on a trip."

"A trip? I can't. I need to go to the courthouse."

"I've already talked to your sister, and she agreed, you need some time away. She's going to be there with them."

"That's not fair to her, I should be there as well."

"It was as much her idea as mine." He watched her wheels turn. She was still on the fence.

"Lydia needs to do this. She told me she feels she let you down."

She reared up in the bed. "That makes no sense. She damn near died for me."

"She's your sister. Your *older* sister. You understand her sense of responsibility better than anyone. What is going to make her feel better after hearing your story?"

"She'd need to take control. She'd need to do something for me."

"That's what she's trying to do, sweetheart. Can you let her?"

"Okay."

He hugged her close and breathed a kiss against her temple. "So it means you're willing to do a favor for me too. I really appreciate it."

Beth laughed at his silliness.

"So where are we going?"

"Vegas, baby."

"Las Vegas?"

"I want to be someplace close so when the team gets back we can discuss the next steps."

"What next steps?"

"For after your father testifies against the DEA agents. Everyone is pretty sure they'll realize they're well and truly caught, and they'll roll and testify against Guzman and the congressman."

Beth nodded, she knew this plan.

"Then they should have the information they need to go after Guzman and finally get him."

She nodded again.

"I want to be able to come back when it happens. Or when the team comes back, whichever comes first. I want to start making plans with the good members of the DEA, US Marshals, and Midnight Delta to take down Guzman. That's why I don't want to be far from California."

Beth shuddered, and he knew the direction her thoughts had taken.

"You can be damn sure when we take down Alfonso, his loyal little son is going down too. Hell, Alberto is nothing but a useless boil on daddy's butt, he's a nothing."

She clutched him.

"Now, you get into the shower, and we're all going to Vegas."

"All?"

"Did you think we weren't taking the swabbies with us? Lou, Mike, Chris and Terry would be disappointed if we left them behind." He got another smile, just what he wanted.

He watched as the nightshirt shifted around her round ass as she made her way to the bathroom. As soon as the door closed, he flopped down on the bed and groaned. He was going to be canonized for sainthood. He hadn't stayed this hard for this long since high school.

The door opened.

"Did you say something?"

"I just coughed." He lied.

"Oh, okay. Maybe some tea with lemon would help," Beth suggested as she closed the door.

Nope, it was not what was needed. *Suck it up, and get dressed, Preston.*

****

Beth was dazed. She'd just walked through an amazing lobby filled with crystals and lights. Everywhere her eyes went were more prisms and sparkles. She'd looked at the men, and they seemed as dazzled as she was. The only person who wasn't was Jack. It was then she realized he'd grown up surrounded by wealth.

They were given key cards to take them high up in the hotel/casino, to a floor containing nothing but suites. When he opened the door, it was amazing. The room was actually two stories.

"This is too much. I've never seen anything like this." Jack laughed.

"This is Mom's favorite place to stay when she and Dad come to Las Vegas. I wanted to bring you here."

"Seriously, how much does this cost? Can't we stay some place not so...well not so luxurious?"

"Don't you like it? My mom likes it. There's even a little elevator for her so she doesn't have to walk up the stairs to the second floor."

She saw the disappointment in his eyes. This was important to him. He'd wanted to give her something special, and she was screwing it up.

"I was wrong, this is fantastic." She hugged him.

"Really?"

"Really." She kissed him. Now she was over her self-consciousness, she had to admit it was stunning. She looked at the huge windows, and she flew across the room and peered down at the busy Las Vegas strip. It was lit up brighter than any Christmas tree she'd ever seen. As a matter of fact, she had to squint to see the people down below.

"Oh my God, what's that, Jack? Look, quick!" Jack came over by her side, put his arm around her, and looked at what she was pointing to.

"Those are the Bellagio Fountains. If you listen really carefully, you can hear the music that goes with the show."

"My God, it's beautiful. Can we go see them?"

"Definitely. I don't think it would be a true trip without seeing one of their shows. Maybe I can get reservations at the restaurant near the fountains and they'll have tables that overlook them."

"Look, Jack, they're changing colors." Beth knew her nose was actually pressed up against the glass of the window like a little kid, but she couldn't help herself.

"Let me make a call." He brushed back her hair and kissed her neck. "If you're this excited seeing it from up here, I can't wait to see the look on your face when we're up close."

Beth shivered at the caress. It was going to be a wonderful night. Then she paused. "Is it really fancy where we're going? I don't have really fancy clothes with me."

"People will be dressed in all different types of clothes. Jeans and T-shirts, shorts, and then there will be others who will look like they're going to the Oscars. Now me, I like to be comfortable in jeans." She breathed a sigh of relief. She could wear a nice pair of black slacks and her pretty blue blouse.

"Jack, I need to call Lydia first."

"I understand. I'm going to call down and see if I can get a reservation. One for us, and one for the guys." She cocked her head.

"They're *not* sitting at our table." She giggled.

When she dialed, she got Lydia's voice mail.

"Hey, give me a call back, I want to know how Papa's first day of testimony went. I hope he's holding up okay. I hope Mama is too. If you need me to come back, just say the word."

Beth went into the master suite to change. She looked at the big bed and shivered. Tonight she and Jack would make love...she hoped. She put on her outfit and kept the top two buttons unbuttoned so it would show off her necklace. She ran her hand over it. It gave her courage.

Jack knocked on the door. "We have reservations."

She came out.

"You look beautiful." He always said that, but she was beginning to think she might be—in his eyes at least.

"How far do we have to walk?"

"We cab it. It's a much further walk than you think. You always cab it in Vegas." He winked at her.

****

Dinner had been fabulous, but now Beth was even more excited to get back to the room. Jack had ordered champagne. She'd only had it once before at a cousin's wedding, and the bubbles were still floating through her system. The man who walked with her to the suite was everything she could ever want, and she wanted him badly.

"I hope you enjoyed dinner," Jack said as he slipped his key card into the suite's door. She waited in the hall with Lou and Mike while Jack checked the room, and then he ushered her in.

They said good-night to the men and finally were alone.

"It was beautiful. I loved the music, and the colors, and the food."

"What about the company?" he teased.

"I loved the company most of all," her voice a whisper. Oh God. Could she do this? She was going to. "Jack, can you kiss me?"

"It would be my pleasure."

He took her hand and walked her over to the large window, and there in front of the sparkling backdrop, he took her into his arms. As soon as his head lowered, all thought of the skyline disappeared. He sipped at her lips, his hands softly caressing her back, but that wasn't what she wanted. She broke free of the kiss and looked into his blue eyes that seemed so much darker than normal.

"What is it, sweetheart?"

"I uhm." His hands stroked up and down her back. She leaned backward, trying to get him to press harder. His eyes narrowed in comprehension.

183

"Do you need more?"

"Yes."

He moved one step closer and shifted so their bodies aligned. Beth sighed with satisfaction.

His hand swept down, and moved over the swell of her bottom. She moaned with delight. His kiss turned carnal. For once she thrust her tongue into his mouth, and he groaned. His grip tightened on her ass as he lifted her closer. She felt the heat of his erection and she arched forward, her body twisting, needing relief.

He broke free of their kiss.

"Are you sure?"

"Oh yes. I'm so sure."

His eyes searched her face, and he must have seen the truth because his expression changed. Gone was the beguiling lover, and instead was a marauding Viking of old. He swung her into his arms and strode into the bedroom.

"Sweetheart, you're sure you're with me in this?"

"Jack..." She trembled in need. "I ache." She began unbuttoning his dress shirt, desperate to feel the heat of his skin. It was as if a switch had finally been thrown, all the love she felt shoved away any lingering fear. All that was left was a desperate sense of wanting.

184

Jack's eyes glittered bright blue, as he yanked back the duvet and lowered her onto the sheet.

"Slow down, we'll get there." He stopped her hands.

"No."

"Beth, seriously, I want to undress you."

"Then do it fast." He shouted out a laugh, and she joined him. What a delight to be here in this moment. All fear gone.

She didn't know how he did it, but somehow her SEAL had them both almost naked. Well she was, he had kept on his briefs. Somehow he knew she wasn't quite ready for everything.

"You're so sexy," he breathed. She glowed under his gaze. To him, she was sexy and wasn't that what really mattered? Her body almost vibrated off the bed with anticipation as his hand lowered. She sighed in relief as skin met skin. He stroked all the way from her collar bone to the outside of her knee, all while watching her carefully.

"Again. Please."

He chuckled. He trailed his palm back up the same path, taking his time, and causing every nerve in her body to come to the surface of her skin. Vaguely she considered touching him but was too greedy. She wanted to concentrate on these feelings, on watching his blue eyes blaze as he looked at her.

She grasped both of his wrists and brought his palms to her breasts. He huffed out a breath that ended on a groan.

"Perfect," he said as he molded her firm, silky flesh in his big hands. Her nipples beaded and she arched off the bed.

"Jack," she wailed. It was so much more than she'd ever imagined. And then his lips were there, and she went higher. Much higher. His knee pressed between her thighs and she eagerly parted her legs in welcome as she clutched his hair. Hair was getting in her eyes, and she realized she was thrashing her head.

"Easy sweetheart, we have all night."

"No, now."

His answer was to gently lap and lave around her areola, bringing her passion down enough to where she could breathe again.

"Beth, you're so beautiful." Lick.

"Feeling you shiver..." Stroke.

"Hearing you sigh..." Caress.

"All of it makes me want to take my time." His diabolical hands cupped her hips holding her in place, and then his tongue made forays in her bellybutton. Beth gasped as she started to climb higher to some nameless place only Jack could take her. She jerked against the restraint of his hands, trying to push closer to his exploring tongue. The sensations he created arrowed straight to her core.

Beth felt her flesh melt in welcome. This time, she needed so much more than before, and she wasn't in the mood for waiting. She smiled a smile as old as time and gripped the hair of her lover, her one love. He lifted up, his eyes held a question.

"Yes?"

"I need more now." His eyebrow lifted. "Pretty please?"

Jack's blue eyes sparkled.

"Oh girl, for you, everything." His broad hands reached around and stroked the backs of her thighs, and then parted her legs. The air wafted against her flesh, and then he was there, sliding through her slick folds until he finally touched her where she most needed him. She moaned her need.

"I have you." And she knew he did. She was safe.

He loved her with his touch, his tongue, his soul and she flew.

****

Jack hovered over Beth as she quivered with spent passion. He could stay like this forever. Her body literally shimmered with an 'other-worldly' glow. She stared at him, her midnight eyes filled with secrets and dreams. Finally, her smile turned wicked.

"Pretty please with sugar on top, now can we can finally make love? Real love? Total love?"

"Try and stop me!" Laughter clear in his voice as he skimmed out of his briefs, and she sucked in her breath.

"My God, Jack. Will this work?"

"Trust me." He sheathed himself in protection as she watched in fascination. He thought he might explode under her gaze.

"Can I touch you?"

"Next time," he rasped.

Jack positioned himself at her portal and continued to watch her. Her focus turned inwards as he moved forward.

"Easy girl." Her hot tight depths clutched him. He saw a frown begin to form, and he moved one hand until it rested above her mound. His thumb brushed through her wet curls and found its engorged target. He began circling the bud.

"Jack," she panted.

"I'm here."

"I noticed." He would have laughed except he was gritting his teeth, intent on staying still. He lifted his hand away, and she moved upwards to follow, sheathing him deeper. His thumb would flutter against her, teasing her, teaching her, until she moved up and down in a tempo making sweat bead on his brow.

"Feels so good." She reached down and grasped his ass, pulling him forward, deeper, her heels rode up his thighs. She was ready.

Jack started, pulled out, and slid back in savoring her sighs. Soon they found the perfect rhythm, and his moans of pleasure melded with her sounds. He touched his forehead to hers. Their eyes met, unveiling all of their needs and wants.

He wanted faster, she needed deeper. His arms reached around and hugged her close as they crashed into to a cacophony of stars, each crying out their joy and their love.

Chapter Thirteen

Beth looked across the small table at Jack and found it hard to believe this man was hers. Every one of her dreams was coming true. They'd been in Las Vegas for five days, and it had been magical.

Today they were going back to California. She had tried to talk to Lydia while she'd been here, but her sister insisted she enjoy her time away. She did get to hear that her father had testified for two days, and the prosecutors thought his testimony would make a difference in the case. Jack held her when she'd cried in relief that it was finally over.

This morning, like every morning before, Jack arranged for their breakfast to be wheeled into their suite. Today was Eggs Benedict and waffles. The table was next to the two story window, and she looked down and saw the hustle and bustle of the Las Vegas strip.

"I can't believe there is so much activity so early in the morning."

"They call New York the city that never sleeps, but I think Vegas is a close second," Jack said.

"I think the guys have enjoyed the time here too." She grinned as she thought of Mike winning at craps. Lou had taught him how to play, and apparently he now had the nickname 'shooter'—whatever that meant. It'd been such a great time for everyone and Beth wanted to come back here as often as possible.

"What has you grinning, sweetheart? Are you finally thinking about gambling?"

"God no! I can't imagine being so frivolous with money."

Jack looked at her and smiled. "What would you like to do with your money instead?"

"I'd like to help some of the children at the orphanage." Beth had written letters to the children yesterday, and she'd gotten some postcards of the fountains to go with them.

"I'm not surprised. You'll probably end up working with my dad on his charities." Beth considered what Jack said, and couldn't imagine it.

"But, we still don't have anything settled when it comes to my future. I don't know if I have to go into hiding because of the Guzmans. Even with Papa's testimony, they aren't sure the DEA agents are going to roll over on Alfonso Guzman."

"Beth, no matter what you'll remain with me."

191

"I don't want you to have to give up your family or your career."

"I would give up everything in a heartbeat if I had to, but I don't."

"I don't understand."

"If I've learned anything growing up at Richard Preston's knee, it's that money and influence matters."

"I've learned that as well. It would be nice if it was used on my behalf for once." She grimaced.

"Sweetheart, everything is going to start working your way. Trust me."

She smiled. "Actually, it already is." She reached across the table and caressed the back of his hand. "Our time together has been wonderful. Sometimes I think it's what has me worried."

"I don't understand."

"It's almost like things are going so well something bad must happen." Jack got up and came around the table to kneel in front of her.

"You're wrong. The bad is behind you. You deserve rainbows and roses. Nobody deserves it more."

"Oh Jack, please don't say that you'll jinx it." He sifted his hand in her hair and placed a kiss on her lips. "There's no such thing. Now, you better get ready and go pack. Our plane leaves soon."

Beth thought it was funny how much she didn't want to stop kissing Jack. She'd grown addicted to him. After she saw Lydia, she knew the first thing she wanted to do when she got to California, and it wasn't going to the beach!

****

Jack felt like shit for telling Beth everything would be okay. It was just she was so happy, he didn't want to do anything to burst her bubble sooner than necessary. After she went into the master suite, he picked up his phone.

'Shooter' had let it slip this morning the Midnight Delta team had been stateside for the last three days. He'd been calling Clint and Mason for four, and gotten their voicemail, so he'd assumed they were still deployed out of the country. God dammit, he'd been had.

Why in the fuck had they been ducking his phone calls? Why hadn't Lydia mentioned Clint was back in town when she and Beth had talked? His head kept telling him they were fellow SEALs and could be trusted, his gut told him to reach out to someone he *knew*.

He'd called Aiden O'Malley three hours ago and gotten his voicemail. Then he'd sent him a 911 text. Aiden called back during breakfast.

Now Jack was calling him back and waited impatiently for Aiden to pick up.

"What the hell, you send a 911 text and then you don't answer?"

"It's complicated," Jack responded.

"Yeah, you have to babysit a beautiful girl and I'm sludging through sludge. Life's so tough for you."

"Where are you? What are you doing?"

"If I told you, I'd have to kill you. What's up my man?"

"I'm being lied to by my new teammates," Jack spit out the last word like it left a bad taste in his mouth.

"Gault's team? Gault himself?"

"Affirmative."

"What the fuck?!"

"My thoughts exactly."

"I thought you were on babysitting duty. How could you be tangled up in something they would be lying to you about?"

"It's a fuck load more complicated than babysitting duty."

"Okay, that was a stupid question. They shouldn't have been lying to you, no matter what you're doing. You're part of the team. I'm done with my deployment. I'm going to ask for leave. Where do I meet you?"

That was why Jack loved his Senior Chief. No more questions than that, just immediate loyalty and help.

"Beth and I will be back in California in four hours. We're flying into San Diego. For the last three days, Gault's team has been back stateside, and I'm going to confront them. You want in?"

"Absolutely. Just tell me when and where."

This time, when Jack got Mason's voicemail, he left a very detailed message, using some very colorful expletives. It still didn't tamp down his anger, but it helped him put on a calm face for Beth.

****

"Hello Lydia," Jack nodded as cordially as he could. Beth noticed and gave him a questioning look as she walked into her sister's home.

"Beth, you look radiant," Lydia enthused.

"I'm leaving Mike and Lou outside. Terry and Chris are going to head home. I have to go for a little bit. I'll be back in a couple of hours."

"Jack, we just got here. Where are you going?"

"I have to check in, sweetheart." Lydia didn't meet his eyes.

"Oh, I didn't think of that." Beth came over and hugged him. "Hurry back."

"I'll be back as quick as I can. Enjoy your time with your sister." Lydia looked pale. Good. She was as accountable as the rest of them. Goddammit, somebody better tell him what the hell was going on, and soon.

He shut the door softly behind him.

"Mason is over at the Denny's down the street," Lou said as he passed him. Jack nodded and got into the SUV.

"Fucking automatic! Can't even grind the gears," Jack groused as he slammed it into drive. He was in the Denny's parking lot in less than five minutes—it should have taken him ten. Mason and Clint were in a booth in the back. They looked grim. They should have looked scared.

"Sit down Preston, you're frightening the natives."

Jack looked around and saw people staring at him, so he sat across from the two men.

"Explain."

"It's complicated," Clint started.

"Uncomplicate it."

Clint slammed his hands on the Formica table top. "Look you asshat, Beth means as much to me as she does to you."

"Bullshit. You wouldn't have kept me in the dark so I couldn't be properly protecting her if she meant something to you. Both of you are so fucking out of line it is beyond comprehension."

"Watch it, Preston," Mason warned.

"Quit acting like you're my lieutenant. You haven't earned my loyalty."

Mason sighed. "From your perspective, I can understand that."

"Jack, we really thought we would have this under control, and you, and especially Beth, would never need to know. After what Lydia told me, I *really* didn't want Beth to ever have to know."

"What did Lydia tell you?" Mason asked.

"Sorry Mase, I can't tell you, it's private," Clint answered.

Jack knew it had to be about the molestation. It meant all of this had to do with Berto.

"Well apparently your plans didn't work, so tell me."

"Nine days ago Guzman senior was captured. Everybody has kept it hush-hush because of everything else we've found."

Jack was trying to wrap his head around everything. If Guzman senior had been captured, it should have meant the Hidalgo's didn't need to go into witness protection. None of them were targets any longer. They only needed protective duty until Ricardo testified, and then they were done. The Hidalgo's were free to live their lives.

"Explain. This should have ended it."

"We said senior has been captured. It looks like Guzman junior has taken the business to new heights, or depths. However, you want to slice it. It's bad." Clint looked at Jack, his face filled with anger and disgust.

"Look, Clint, just tell me. I'm tired of the guessing games."

"Berto Guzman is in the human trafficking business. It's a big time operation. DHS, DEA, and our team are all working to stop this bastard. When we broke into Guzman senior's location, we found the information on one shipment. They're moving the people in shipping containers. We debriefed some of the women. Apparently Berto is making use of the women before selling them off. He is targeting specific types—all Hispanic." Clint's voice trailed off. Both men sat in the booth opposite Jack, and they looked at him with sympathy.

Jack felt almost as sick as when Beth told her story of abuse at Berto's hands when she'd been a teenager.

"So the bastard is obsessed with Beth," Jack surmised. "All of the girls look like her, right?"

"You got it in one," Mason agreed. "We've been trying to figure out if he ever met her. Clint told me recently he had. He won't tell me the details, but he said it was a significant encounter."

"Yeah, you could say that," Jack said bitterly.

"Jack, you gotta understand, we really thought by this time we would have Berto caught along with his father. Then Beth would be able to live free and clear along with Lydia and her parents. That's all we wanted for her." Jack heard the faint plea in Clint's voice, but he didn't give a shit. He should have been told. Mason must have seen what he was thinking.

"This was my call, not Clint's. If anyone is to blame it's me, Preston."

"And you're who I'm holding at fault. This wouldn't have happened with my lieutenant." Jack got up.

"Hold up, where are you going?"

"I'm headed back to Beth."

"We'll meet you there. We'll have a team meeting, and bring you up to speed."

"It doesn't sound like you've gotten very far."

"Don't be too sure."

"I'm bringing in one of my teammates."

"Who?" Mason demanded.

"Aiden O'Malley." Jack stared at both men. He felt the eyes of some of the patrons and realized he was once again causing a stir. He really didn't care.

"I know him. He's a good man." Jack didn't say anything.

"When will he be available?" Mason asked.

"He'll be here within the hour." He had to get the hell out of there. If he didn't, he'd say something he'd regret. Despite everything, there was a part of him that understood why they'd done it, and he respected them for it. He would have tried to protect Beth as well in their shoes.

****

"Let me get this straight. You got engaged, officially engaged, while I was in Las Vegas? There was an actual party with hundreds of people and I wasn't invited?" Beth thought her head might explode.

Lydia looked like she was going to cry.

"I didn't know about the party, it was a surprise, and there weren't hundreds of people, I promise."

"Oh for God's sake, it doesn't matter if there were hundreds or ten. Mama and Papa were there, and people you cared about. Just not me. You never mentioned once on any call that Clint was back in town for three days. Then after the party, you never told me about it. I can't believe you!" Beth took a deep breath. "Now let me look at the ring again." Beth grabbed Lydia's hand. Not sure if she wanted to slap it or cry.

"It was a surprise. If I'd known about the party, I would have invited you."

"Clint should have invited me. What the hell is going on? And don't tell me nothing!" Beth was having none of the lies. "You know, Lydia, we've played some weird games in our little lives. You protect me, I bully you."

"And it works," Lydia exclaimed.

"You've needed to be bullied because you damn well don't take care of yourself, but I haven't needed protection for quite some time."

Lydia gave her a pointed look.

"See! See that look." Beth's eyes watered. "I was scared to death in the jungle, but why did it have to be you? Why did you have to be the martyr? To this day, I regret I let you take the beating. I should have been stronger. You never protect yourself."

"Beth, I love you. I want to take care of you."

"I know you do, and something is up, and you're protecting me again." Beth started to cry. "The price was too high in the jungle and it's too high now. I didn't get to see you on your happiest day. What? You're going to protect me again, and I won't get to see you on your wedding? I won't get to be there for the birth of your first child?"

"No! God, no!" Lydia tried to hug her, but Beth shoved her away. "Please Beth, let me explain."

"It's too late."

"I was just trying..." Lydia stopped short.

"You were trying to protect me," Beth finished bitterly.

"It's bad. It's really bad."

"So tell me. I'm a big girl. Hell, do you know how many times *I've* had to be the big sister? Do you realize how many times I've pushed you around? Think about it, Lydia. Really think about it."

Beth watched the comprehension dawn on Lydia's face. Good. She was sick of this. She *wanted*—no—she *needed* to be treated as an equal. They both did, it was the only way this relationship was ever going to work.

"Alfonso Guzman was captured over a week ago. It was when you were in Texas." Beth just waited. Obviously, it wasn't the good news it should have been.

"So tell me the rest," Beth demanded.

"Berto's taken over a new part of the operation." Beth winced at the mention of the man's name. Lydia again tried to put her arms around her.

"Not yet, you don't get to hug me yet. Just finish it."

"Berto is embroiled in human trafficking, and what's worse is he's targeting girls who look like you." Beth slumped, and this time, when Lydia went to hug her, she let her.

"That's what you didn't want to tell me," she whispered.

"Oh baby girl, we thought, Clint and Mason thought, he would be captured by now. And you would never have to know."

"You can't leave me in the dark anymore. You just can't," she said in a raspy whisper.

203

"I see that now. Please forgive me."

Beth looked into her sister's brown eyes. They were still wet with tears.

"Are we clear we're not going to do this stupid 'protect each other thing'? We're going to be equals?"

"Equals who care and support one another. But Beth, sometimes I do need to be bullied."

Beth gave a soggy laugh.

"Yeah, you do. But from now on it's Clint's job."
Beth sniffed and wiped her eyes. "Let me see the ring again."

****

Beth waited for Jack out on the stoop of the duplex. She'd seen Lou and Mike across the street earlier. They'd waved to her, and she gave them a half-hearted wave back.

"Beth, why are you out here?" Jack asked as he made his way up the stairs. "Have you been crying?"

"Yeah. I'm over it." He sat down beside her.

"Is Lydia still inside?"

"Yeah. I saw you pulling up." She gave a big sigh. "So was your meeting to talk to Clint?"

"Yeah." He put his arm around her shoulders and coaxed her head against him. "It's a pretty fucked up situation," he said.

She snorted.

"I got that. I think what burns me the most is I missed the engagement party."

"What engagement party?"

"Clint proposed to Lydia, he threw a surprise engagement party. We missed it. I know they thought they would have captured Berto, but it still makes me mad."

"Join me on the angry train." He kissed the top of her head. "He's an asshole for having the party without you, but there was a good reason why he's kept you away. He's coming over here right now with the rest of the team to fill us in."

"At least, Lydia didn't know about it, so *she* didn't exclude me."

"That's good. Let's get back inside. I see Mason and Clint parking right now." She saw the two men getting out of Clint's truck. Jack held out his hand to her. She took it, and he guided her inside.

Chapter Fourteen

Beth sat close to Jack on the couch. Lydia and Clint were seated on the loveseat across from them, and Mason stood near the front door as they waited for members of the team to arrive.

"I'm really sorry about keeping the two of you in the dark. It was a mistake on my part."

She looked at Jack and saw him give Mason a nod. It looked like maybe things would work out. She hoped so. No matter what, she would always remember how Mason and his team had saved her and her family.

"Mason, Aiden will be here in fifteen minutes," Jack reported after looking at his phone.

"I think he is going to be a good addition to this project." She felt Jack relax even more.

There was a knock on the door, and Mason opened it. It was Finn Crandall. He'd been on the protection detail with her parents, and she hadn't seen him in months. She knew he'd come close to losing his life when her parents were almost killed.

He came and squatted in front of her. "Beth, it's good to see you."

"You too. Thank you for being such a good friend to Mama. She told me how you brought her romance books."

Mason laughed.

"How are you?"

"Fine."

"How are you really?"

"Stressed and concerned."

"Fair enough." He stood up and grabbed a couple of chairs from the dining room and positioned them around the living room before sitting in one. Next came Darius, he too came up to Beth.

"You're looking even better now. I'd say Las Vegas agreed with you more than even Texas." He smiled. She couldn't help but smile back.

"Hang in there, kid. We're going to get this bastard." Jack tensed beside her and she looked at him.

"It's nothing, sweetheart." She kissed his jaw. Beth watched as Darius went to sit beside Finn. There was a knock on the door and Mason let in a man she didn't recognize.

"Jack!"

"Aiden!"

Jack gave her a squeeze, crossed the room, and shook hands with the man. He was older than any of the other men. He looked angry when he turned to Mason.

"So what kind of happy horseshit has been going on here, Lieutenant?"

"Senior Chief, if you're going to be an insubordinate asshole you can leave. If you're going to be a support to your friend, you can stay."

The door opened, and Drake walked in.

"Who's the insubordinate asshole, Mase? I thought it was my role."

"Not now, Drake," Mason said in a no nonsense tone.

"I've talked to one of the most outstanding men I've ever had the pleasure to serve with twice today. He's told me you have been dicking around on the security detail of his assignment. I don't know which woman this is, I'm assuming it's this girl here." He pointed at Beth.

"Aiden, I really need you to tone it down," Jack asked.

The man looked around the room. It was clear he was used to giving orders, not taking them. He considered what both men said.

"Okay, fill me in."

"First things first." Mason came over and sat on the other side of her. "Beth, I hope you will accept my sincere apology."

"I can't. First I have to know the whole thing. Lydia's told me a lot, but I'm betting there's more." He nodded.

"Guzman has been captured, but Berto is still out there. He's running a human trafficking ring. We thought we could capture him before your father testified. We didn't want to tell you he was out there. Beth, I don't know how to tell you this."

"He still wants me," she said softly. "It's okay. I guessed." Mason looked at her questioningly. Jack cupped her cheek and turned her head so she was looking at him.

"How did you guess, sweetheart?"

"At the cabin, one of the men said I had to be kept alive for the boss. I knew, in my heart, it was Berto. I knew he'd never forgotten me."

"That fucker!" Lydia shouted.

209

"It's okay, Lydia," Beth tried to soothe her sister.

"It's not."

"I don't understand," Drake said.

"You explain it, Lydia, I can't." Beth clutched Jack's hand.

Clint stroked his hand down Lydia's back as she stood up and made her way to the middle of the room. She looked around at all of the men and then her eyes finally rested on her baby sister. Beth nodded.

"Aiden, you're coming in cold to this operation, so I'm going to talk to you," Lydia said. "Berto, is Alfonso Guzman's son. He started a human trafficking ring a year ago. We found out he's been choosing women from these groups who look like my sister and taking them for his own. They're never heard from again. We didn't know if Berto had ever met my sister, but she told me recently he molested her when she was sixteen."

"What the fuck?!" Drake turned to Beth. "The little fucking animal laid hands on you when you were a baby?"

Beth started at Drake's sharp words and leaned closer into Jack's warmth.

"Ah shit, Beth. I didn't mean to scare you, kid. But the motherfucker touched you?" This time, he said it softly and sadly. She nodded.

210

"He's got to die."

"You called it. And I'm pulling the trigger, are we clear?" Jack's voice rumbled beneath her.

"Abso-fucking-lutely," Drake agreed.

"Gentlemen, before we call dibs on who gets to take him out, we need to figure out how to find the bastard. Remember there are at least thirty people working this case. There is no guarantee we're going to be the ones who take him down," Mason pointed out.

"Oh, it's going to be us," Jack's tone would have scared her if his arms weren't holding her so gently. "So, what exactly do we know? What's being done?" Jack asked.

"Most of the people being sold are women."

"You mean they all aren't?" Beth asked as she watched Lydia sit down next to Clint and rest her head against his shoulder. Clint brushed a kiss on her hair.

"No, some are being used for migrant crop work, but the vast majority are women," Mason said. "They're coming through the Mexico City Valley. That's where we found them when we took down Guzman."

"Were they on their way to the United States?" Aiden asked.

211

"That's what DHS thinks, and it's why they were all over this operation when the DEA reported it," Mason responded.

"Likely they were headed to Laredo, then all points north," Aiden said.

"That's what they surmised," Mason concurred.

"I know what the DEA is. What is the DHS?" Beth asked.

"Department of Homeland Security. They take this really seriously, sweetheart." Jack explained to her.

"Mason, how many people do you think Berto has kidnapped?" she asked.

"We really don't know. We know he's been in operation for at least a year." She pressed her hand over her stomach.

"Where does he get these people? Are they from Mexico? How do they transport them?" Mason got up from the couch walked past Aiden, who was now seated in one of the dining room chairs, and stood next to Drake.

"Beth, it isn't pretty," he finally answered.

"Just tell me, Mason. It can't be any worse than what they did to Lydia in the shack."

He nodded.

"The people they are getting from outside of Mexico, they're transporting in shipping containers on cargo ships." Beth was thankful she hadn't had any food.

"Where are they coming from? How long is the trip?"

"Sometimes from Asia. Sometimes from South America. We're not quite sure how long they're locked up in the containers. It depends on the shipping route."

"Beth, Clint, and I have been working with our contacts, and doing some of our own searches. We have some leads DHS doesn't," Lydia said pointing to the desk in the corner that housed, at least, four computers and monitors.

"Have you been working with Rylie? Has Rylie shown up again and you haven't told me?" Darius barked out the question. Lydia didn't seem surprised.

"Yes, I actually got a transmission from her. Even though Alfonso and his gang of drug runners have been put out of business, Berto seems to be using the same tactics to keep people in line."

"Oh God, not the same kind of torture. And Rylie has actually watched some of that shit?" Darius sounded appalled. "I thought you were going to tell me when she contacted you."

"Back off, Dare. We just heard from her yesterday," Clint said. "We're telling you now." Clint pulled Lydia back down beside him.

"Were you able to track her down further than the boonies of Oklahoma this time?" Darius demanded.

"Not yet, we're still working on it," Lydia said.

"Who is Rylie? Can she really help us?" Beth asked.

"She's a woman with more daring than sense," Darius bit out. "She's almost your age, Beth. She faked her own death when she as seventeen, and she's been off the grid ever since. Now she dabbles in some of the scariest shit imaginable."

"I don't understand."

"She's a hacker," Lydia explained. "She gets a lot of information. I think she's used her skills to get money for some of the kids she used to be in foster care with. We have evidence she arranged for donations to a home for abused and neglected children."

"So she's robbing people," Beth said.

"No, she's not a thief. Not exactly," Darius defended. "Explain it to her Lydia."

"When I did some digging, I found out she was funneling funds from people like Guzman."

"Which is horrifying. Can you imagine what would happen if she got caught? Someone needs to rein her in." Darius looked like he might burst a blood vessel.

"Let's get back on track. What did the transmission tell you?" Jack asked.

"It was one of the normal ones if you can call this kind of thing normal," Clint grimaced. "One of Berto's former men was getting cut as a warning to others. He had apparently abused some of the merchandise."

Beth had an idea of what the terms 'cut', 'abused', and 'merchandise' meant, and once again she was feeling ill. This time, when Jack tried to pull her closer, she didn't let him. Her body was too rigid, and she couldn't be soothed.

"The good news is we got some close-ups of the victim's gang tattoos, and he is out of Veracruz. We'd been thinking they would be operating out of the Port of Lazardo Cardenas because of the Asia connection, but it looks like they're using the Gulf of Mexico instead."

"That is good news," Aiden said.

"I agree with O'Malley. Great work, Clint. You too, Lydia," Mason complimented. "The question is, do we tell DHS and DEA? Right now they're focused on Cardenas."

"Hell Mason, it could be the Pacific side as easily as the Atlantic. We're not sure this information is a good lead," Clint said as he rubbed Lydia's shoulder. "We just don't know. We need more intel."

"Yeah but, Clint, which one do you think it is? What does your gut tell you?"

"Veracruz. Lydia and I are working all of our contacts."

"Not all of them," Aiden said. "All of my mother's people are from the Yucatan Peninsula. I can't tell you how much time I've spent down there, I'm practically a native." Beth really looked at the man and realized despite his Anglo name, and light eyes, he looked a huge Mayan warrior.

"Veracruz isn't on the Yucatan Peninsula," Drake protested.

"It's close enough. If I go down there, especially if I have family with me, I'll get answers about Berto's new business."

"Then we have a plan," Mason said with satisfaction.

"Good, because I ordered pizza. It should be here any minute. I'm starved." Beth stared at Drake. The man was unbelievable.

****

"Dammit Drake, you never order sides or wings. What the fuck is your problem?" Finn groused.

Drake put the eight pizza boxes on the dining room table.

"I bought you your damn lunch, what more could you ask for?"

"I just told you—wings." The men gathered around the dining room table. Beth couldn't imagine eating a bite. Lydia sat next to her on the couch.

"I can't believe these guys. I thought Aiden was going to punch Mason," Lydia said.

"He seemed like a hot head."

"That's one way to put it," Lydia said as she rolled her eyes.

"Beth, are we good?"

Beth put her arm around her big sister. "I'm still disappointed about the engagement party, but I intend to torture Clint about it for the next year. It's not your fault."

Lydia smiled. "I'm good with that."

"There sure is a lot of testosterone in this room."

"It's kind of yummy."

Beth blushed.

"Our guys are the yummiest," Lydia teased.

Beth looked at the dining room table where they were loading up their plates. She had to admit, Clint and Jack sure looked good. Jack looked the best, though.

"Do you want something to eat?" Lydia asked.

"I can't. This has been a lot to take in."

Clint broke away from the group and came over.

"I'm going to go get some beer, do you want anything, Lydia?" Clint held up the keys to his truck.

"Let me go. Beth and I need some space." Beth practically jumped off the couch.

"That's a great idea."

Lydia grabbed the keys out of Clint's hand.

Jack came over.

"We'll go with you."

"Oh for God's sake. Mike and Lou are outside. They'll follow us to the store. It's just down the street. I go every other day." Lydia laughed at the two men, then she kissed Clint on his chin. He smiled.

Jack put his arms around Beth and kissed her forehead.

"Don't forget to get some Shiner Bock."

"Pacifico for me," Clint said. "Do you need cash?"

"I'm covered," Lydia said as she grabbed Beth's hand. "Let's go before they change their minds and decide to go with us."

Lydia had them out of the house and down the front stairs before Beth could blink. It felt good to be in the fresh air. The sisters waved to Mike and Lou, who started up their SUV as the girls stepped into Clint's truck.

"If I didn't know Clint so intimately, I would think he was compensating for something with the size of his truck." Lydia giggled.

Beth blushed.

"That's the second time you've blushed in five minutes. I wouldn't think you still could after all the time in Vegas," Lydia said as she backed out of the driveway.

"What do you mean?"

"You don't think I really wanted to make a beer run for the guys, do you? I couldn't care less if they had their Pacifico. I wanted to find out all the details about you and Jack."

Lydia adjusted the rear view mirror and then cut a sideways glance at Beth.

"We're going to take a hell of a long time at the supermarket, and you're going to tell me every little detail."

Beth smiled. Before all the drama, she'd really been looking forward to sharing with Lydia.

"Yay, a smile not a blush. I knew the time alone with Jack was going to be great for you."

"Look out!" Beth screamed as she saw a van pull out in front of them from a side street. Lydia yanked the steering wheel hard to the right and slammed on the brakes. The truck went into a skid as it fishtailed, coming to a stop a couple of feet away from the van. Both women were thrown painfully against their seatbelts, but the airbags didn't deploy.

Beth heard a crash behind her, and she whirled around to see another van hit the car Mike and Lou were in.

Lydia screamed, "Get down."

Beth turned to the front and saw two men with guns had gotten out of the van in front of them. Her heart froze as she heard two shots behind her. Mike and Lou had been shot, she knew it. Lydia leaned over in front of her, opening the glove box. She saw the blue-black metal of a gun, and she slapped Lydia's hand away, knowing what she had to do as the two men advanced.

She grabbed the gun and shoved it up against her throat.

"Beth, what are you doing?" Lydia demanded as she lunged for her, and Beth turned and glared at her.

"They want me. They shot Mike and Lou. They'll shoot you too. I'll threaten to kill myself unless they let you go, and I'll save your life."

"No, God no, Beth!" Lydia wailed, as she clawed at her seatbelt.

"You hurt my sister and I will kill myself," Beth yelled out through the open window.

The two men halted.

"Beth, please don't do this."

"Lydia, undo my seatbelt. This is your only chance. *Our* only chance." She peered sideways at Lydia and saw her considering her words, and then felt her slowly unbuckling her belt.

"Now lean over and open my door."

"Please don't ask me to do this. It's too much."

"Do it."

Lydia was crying. "I can't."

"You know you have to. Now do it." The gun was much heavier than she expected. Her hand was trembling. *God don't let me drop it.* "Please Lydia, open the door, I'm begging you." She was going to start crying, and then it would all be over.

"You two behind us, go join your friends," Lydia yelled.

Beth hadn't even thought about the men who shot Lou and Mike. They waited until two more men walked around to the front of Clint's truck. Now there were four men in front of Beth and Lydia, all staring at the women.

"Look, we want Beth Hidalgo," a big ugly man said with a thick accent. "We don't care about you, bitch."

"Yes, you do. You don't want any witnesses." The first two men exchanged glances.

"Here's what's going to happen," Beth yelled out the window. "I'm going to get out of the truck. I'm going to continue to hold the gun to my throat." Her hand trembled, it was hard to yell with the gun pressed against her neck, but she managed. "My sister is going to drive away. If you try to stop her or rush up to me while she is still here, I will kill myself."

"You won't do it," the first man sneered.

"I will do anything to protect my sister, and you don't want to risk angering Berto. He's crazy, and we all know what he does to people who make him mad."

222

Beth brought her other hand up to help steady the gun.

"Open the door, Lydia." Lydia finally did.

"I'll bring help," she whispered.

"I know you will, remember we're a team."

Beth stood in front of the men as Lydia drove away.

As soon as the truck turned the corner, it was like all of her strength deserted her, and her arms dropped like wet noodles to her side.

"Get her," commanded the first man who'd been doing all the talking.

Chapter Fifteen

The world went quiet around Jack as he watched Clint wave his arm to get everybody to quiet down.

"Are you all right? Answer the fucking question." Clint put his phone on the dining room table and hit speaker.

"Yes, I'm fine. They have Beth. You have to come here now. I'm pretty sure they killed Lou and Mike."

"Where are you?"

"I'm on 5th and McNichols. Oh God, Clint, I can see Mike and Lou in the SUV, there's so much blood. You have to call an ambulance. They told me to drive home, but I didn't, I'm around the corner. They're getting into their vans now. They hit Beth, she's unconscious."

As soon as she said the cross streets, Jack and the others started out the door.

"Keep her talking, Clint. We'll get to her," Mason commanded.

Clint looked ill, but he nodded. Jack remembered his job was intel and communications.

They took three vehicles. Jack drove with Mason, and they drove straight to Lydia's position. The others went to scout where the take-down happened. Lydia was still behind the wheel of Clint's truck on her cell phone. It was clear she wasn't even aware of their presence.

"Lydia," Mason called out as he neared the driver's side of the truck. She finally looked at them. She dropped the phone. They could hear Clint yelling through the tinny speaker.

"Archer, we're here," Mason shouted. "Lydia's fine." He opened the door, and Lydia slumped into his arms.

"You've got to go get Beth. Get her!" She turned to Jack. "They have her Jack. You have to go and save her."

"Tell us what happened." He saw Aiden sprinting around the corner towards them. He was shaking his head. *Fuck. Lou and Mike must be dead.*

"It was a professional hit," Aiden said as he reached him. He wanted to go and see for himself, but he knew his best source of information was Lydia. He looked at the woman, who so closely resembled Beth, as she tried to calm herself. She clutched at Mason, her face ravaged by tears.

225

"They hit her so hard. I don't understand, you know they wanted her alive, why did they hit her, Mason?"

"I thought she had the gun to her head? How did you see them hit her?" Jack still wasn't clear on how this whole event went down.

"I drove away and turned the corner. I parked and watched. That's where I called Clint from." She stopped and tried to collect herself. "That's when I saw Beth drop the gun. All I can figure is it got too heavy for her." She looked at Jack and started to cry again. "Oh God, then the man who'd done all the talking came up and backhanded her so hard she crashed to the ground. For a second, I thought they killed her, but then she moved. They picked her up and shoved her into the van and drove off."

Jack could see everything she'd described in his mind's eye.

"Which way did they go, Lydia?" Mason asked.

"They were going on McNichols Street."

"East or West?" She gave him a helpless look.

"Towards the ocean?" Jack asked.

"Yes, towards the ocean," Lydia answered. Aiden was relaying the information into his cell phone, and so was Mason. Jack heard sirens.

"Come on folks, we need to get out of here," Mason said.

"Don't we have to talk to the police? Aren't I a witness?" Lydia asked.

"Some other time. Not now." Mason got into Clint's truck with Lydia, and Aiden drove with Jack back to the duplex.

"We'll get her back," Aiden promised as he put Mason's truck into gear.

Jack stayed silent.

"Mason and his team are good," Aiden said after being met by Jack's silence. "They might have ducked the police, but I heard Drake and Darius already talking to Clint. He's wired into SDPD, and there's an All-Points Bulletin out on your girl. Clint is working to pull in video feeds from the nearest grocery stores and gas stations so he can get license plates and vehicle descriptions of the vans."

Just two more minutes to the house, and then he could see for himself what was being done, Jack assured himself.

"Are you listening to me? These bastards aren't going to get far. Beth is going to be fine."

"They killed Mike and Lou. They took her in broad daylight," Jack whispered. Aiden finally shut up.

A car Jack didn't recognize almost rammed them as they pulled into the driveway. He and Aiden slammed out of the car, Aiden getting to Terry before Jack had a chance to explain.

"Jack!" Terry cried out. "Is it true?" the man yelled, trying to duck past Aiden.

"Is he cleared?" Aiden demanded.

"He's clear," Jack yelled to Aiden. "Yes, it's true. Get inside." Jack ignored Terry's shocked expression and sped up the stairs. The door was locked, he pounded on it. It slowly opened, and Clint stood there with a gun in his hand.

"Get in." Clint gestured with his free hand.

The three men piled into the house. It didn't seem like the same place he'd been thirty minutes ago before his world had fallen apart.

"Where's Lydia?" They heard the distinctive rumble of Clint's truck, and Clint opened the door and was down the steps before anyone could blink. Jack prowled over to Clint's desk area that had two laptops and three desktop monitors running. He felt Aiden behind him.

"Geez, what kind of set-up is this?"

"Clint does communications for Midnight Delta." One screen held nothing but lines of code. Another screen was divided into twelve sections, each showing a different view of San Diego traffic. One of the laptops actually showed the border crossing into Tijuana.

"Lydia, sit down before you fall down," Clint said. Jack saw Clint urging Lydia to sit on the couch.

"Jack, get out of my way," Lydia said as she made her way to the desk with the computers.

"Baby, you can't mean to work now." She whirled around and shoved her finger into Clint's chest.

"Fuck yes, I'm going to hit the computer now. This is my sister's life we're talking about. Now sit your ass down and help me. I'm calling Melvin. You try to get ahold of Rylie." She glanced at the screens. "Did you pull the supermarket parking lot surveillance footage?"

"It's not online."

Lydia looked up from the computers. "Terry!" she yelled at the young petty officer.

"Yes, Ma'am."

"Get over to the Ralph's grocery store," her voice trailed off. She looked at Clint then at Mason, helplessly. Everybody realized Terry probably wouldn't get what they needed fast enough. Mason pulled out his phone.

"Drake. Go over to the Ralph's grocery store. I think it's on 5th or 6th. I need you to get the parking lot surveillance video for the last two hours. According to Clint, their video isn't on-line. Coordinate with Clint and Lydia on any other places you see with surveillance. They'll tell you if they can tap it or if you have to sweet-talk the owners to give it to you."

Jack liked the plan. There was nobody better to either sweet-talk or intimidate people into providing what was needed than Drake Avery.

"I only got the first three letters of the one van, Clint. I'm so sorry. When I went around the corner it was too far away to see it."

"Those first three letters help, baby. You did great." Clint's hand trembled as he adjusted the monitor so Lydia could see it better for her height. Jack shoved his hands in his pocket, knowing his hands were probably trembling too.

"This is all well and good. But I'm not happy standing around with my thumb up my ass while the geek squad tries to come up with answers," Aiden said to Mason.

"I agree. We know they headed West on McNichols. There is an on-ramp to the Five Freeway north when you head that way."

"We know, it's the camera we're checking," Clint said as his fingers flew over the keyboard, bringing up live feeds of the San Diego Freeway.

Jack watched as Lydia continued to dial a person on Skype. Finally, she got through.

"Hello, my Kitten, what do I owe the pleasure of an actual face to face Skype session. I thought we were going to do voice only from now on?"

Jack looked at the man who was in his mid to late twenties. He was a little on the doughy side, and he could benefit from some training.

"Melvin, I don't have time for your shit."

He must have read the strain in her voice and demeanor because he sat up straight.

"Lydia, what's wrong?"

"Beth. Berto Guzman kidnapped Beth an hour ago. I need to know how he plans to get her out of the area."

"Got it." The screen went blank.

"What the fuck!" Jack pounced forward. He reached for the mouse Lydia had been using, but Clint stopped him.

"Back off, Preston."

"No. I'm part of this, and I will not be told to back off."

"He's right, Clint." Lydia looked at him. "Just don't touch my mouse, okay?" She grinned at him weakly.

231

"Look Melvin logged off because he's going to work his contacts. He'll be calling back as soon as he finds something. He's odd as hell, but he's a great hacker."

"Lydia, do we really have time to deal with freaks and oddballs? We need the A-Team," Jack said seriously.

"You're reading this wrong. He's not a freak," Lydia started.

"He's a freak," Clint inserted. "But his information is gold." Jack switched his attention to Clint.

"Fine. Let me know when you get something." He turned to see Mason and Aiden at the dining room table, Mason motioned him over.

"What have you got?"

"Drake talked to a clerk at the gas station near the freeway entrance. The two vans took the south entrance to the freeway. We've notified the border."

"Let's go."

****

It stank.

Oh God, she couldn't see. Her eyes were wide open, but she couldn't see.

"Help!" her voice echoed. She was lying on something hard. She couldn't see. "Hello! Is anyone here?" she yelled louder than before. She tried to sit up, but her hands slipped. She was lying in about a half-inch of warm water. It felt oily. She tried to push off the floor again, but her hands slipped out from under her, and she landed hard against her shoulder.

Beth grunted in pain. She couldn't see anything. She wished her sense of smell had gone away along with her sight. It smelled of oil, piss, and shit. She prayed her hands were only in oily water, but by the smell, she wasn't so sure. Finally, she was able to get onto her hands and knees.

"Hello?" Again, just the eerie echo. She didn't think she was blind, probably in someplace where it was completely dark. *Think Beth!*

It all came flooding back. She'd been driving with Lydia. They'd almost crashed into a van. Lou and Mike! Her hand slipped in the slime as she remembered the shots. She trembled. Please let Lydia have gotten away safely.

She wanted to scream. To cry. To beg someone for help. She bit her lip to stop herself from crying out Jack's name. It was so stupid. She whispered it. Whispered it again. Finally, she calmed down and she could think.

She stayed still. She could feel and hear a slight rumbling. Underneath her, the floor was moving. She was in some kind of moving vehicle. Despite the dampness of her clothes, she wasn't cold. It was hot, which added to the smelly misery.

Suddenly the floor under her lurched, and once again Beth slipped, this time her cheek hit the floor and fiery pain exploded. Another memory formed. She had been hit in the face by a man.

Now she could see bright shards of colorful lights, but they weren't real, just bursts exploding through her pain filled brain. She worked hard to get back up on her hands and knees, and this time she started to crawl. She had to find something to lean against. There had to be a wall somewhere. Beth moved slowly, the last thing she wanted to do was bang her head against the side of whatever she was in.

She tried to block out the smells, but also to listen. She thought she heard whining. What was that? It sounded like something she should recognize. Her shoulder ran into something hard. She reached out with her hand and found steel with rivets.

A shipping container? Was she in one of the cargo containers they shipped the girls in? *Keep it together.* She reached up and felt under her blouse, there it was the necklace—the one Grace had given her. She took a breath, through her mouth, and whispered Jack's name again. Okay, she was doing better.

She needed to sit up and rest, and then she could start planning. She maneuvered herself against the wall, and finally had enough courage to sniff her hand. Thank God, only oil. If this was a shipping container, then there was probably some kind of bucket to use as a toilet and that's the reason for the stench. Why was she in here by herself?

Were they sending her overseas? That didn't make any sense. They would be getting her to Berto somehow. The container lurched again, and her cheek hurt even though it didn't bang against anything. She felt around her body, and finally felt the back of her collar was dry, so she wiped her hands off, and then she started to probe her face. Her right side was definitely swollen. A lot. Even her eye was swollen, but she could open it. She finally saw light coming through tiny pinholes high above. Probably ten feet from the floor of the crate.

Then Beth recognized the whine, it was the sounds she'd heard on the freeway of a truck braking and shifting gears. She was on a truck. What happened to the van? How long was she unconscious? She rested her head against the side of the container, and it jerked slamming her head against the side. Oh no, not again, she thought as she drifted into unconsciousness.

****

The vans had been found in Temecula five hours ago. It was obvious Beth was being transported over the border. It had taken every ounce of patience Jack had not to drive to Tijuana, but he knew it wouldn't accomplish a damn thing. He needed intel. Clint and Lydia were the best he'd ever seen working their contacts. Mason had everyone lined up to go at a moment's notice.

The Melvin character just pinged and said he'd be Skyping in five minutes. They stood around the desk full of computer monitors. Lydia's phone rang, she looked down and sucked in a loud breath.

"Fuck, it's Rylie."

"Put it on speaker," Darius demanded.

"Rylie, can you do a three-way Skype with Melvin?" Lydia asked.

"Yep." The line went dead.

Jack was getting sick of the way these people just hung up. The monitors lit up. Doughboy and a pretty young blonde filled the screens.

"What have you got?" Jack demanded.

"Who's the Viking?" Melvin asked.

"He belongs to Beth. Shut up and answer his question," Lydia snapped.

Rylie and Melvin started talking at the same time, but Jack could understand them. Rylie was explaining Berto was in Veracruz, and there was a big problem with the operation. He was literally slicing and dicing employees to get them back in line. Melvin was ' saying he had found a small trucking operation leading out of the US of specialty types of product being sold to the Middle East. He suspected Beth had been transported on a truck.

"Where are you getting your information?" Jack demanded.

"I found a site on the dark web. It's a little like finding a Russian bride, only it allows you to buy a woman."

Jack looked at the man on the screen and saw he was serious.

"How do you know the women are coming from the US?"

"I did a cross-reference to the missing person's sites here in the US and found correlations. The only thing I don't know is if this is Berto's operation."

"Shit."

"I *do* know my information relates to Berto," Rylie spoke up. The woman who looked like she should be a sophomore in college.

"Don't tell me you found more of those fucking videos, Rylie," Darius said.

"Fine, I won't."

237

"Why does the bastard keep posting them?"

"That's his way of keeping his men in line, and it's pretty Goddamn effective. He beheaded this last guy after cutting out his tongue for snitching to the authorities. Once again the butcher was tatted up with Veracruz gang tattoos."

"But you said Berto was in Veracruz, what makes you think that?"

"You could actually hear him in the background."

"How do you know it was him, Rylie?" Darius asked in an ominous tone of voice.

The woman looked uncomfortable.

"Rylie, answer the fucking question!"

"I met him once! Okay?" Jack looked at her, trying to wrap his head around how this girl could have met a notorious slave trader.

"Explain yourself fast, Rylie," Darius said in a low tone. "How in the fuck do you know Berto Guzman?"

"It was when I was acting as Sylvia. I was working a con on his father to get money for one of the charities. I was in Laredo—it wasn't in Mexico. I didn't expect either of them to actually show up. I was working on their banker at a charity benefit."

"Jesus."

"It's okay. I got out of there quicker 'n snot."

Lydia told Jack earlier Rylie sometimes took on the persona of Sylvia Hessman when she went out in person.

"Okay, so we know Berto is in Veracruz," Jack said.

"Rylie, we are *so* going to talk about your habits," Darius said.

"Shut up, Darius," Jack damn near yelled at the other man. "She got us valuable information. Beth is probably going to end up in Veracruz."

"Or Berto could come out to the West Coast and meet up with her here," Lydia said.

"Not likely," Rylie disagreed. "This is a big problem he has in his Veracruz operation, and he's needed there. He's going to have your sister delivered there."

"I'm not so sure. Melvin, what do you think?" Lydia asked the other person on the video screen.

"I think there is a whole set up here on the West Coast for US girls. It looks like he ships them from here to overseas. Why transport her overland to the East coast of Mexico, when he can just hop a flight to Tijuana?"

"We're splitting up," Jack decided. "Aiden and I are going to Veracruz. We're going to meet up with some

239

of his family from the Yucatan. They can help us search Veracruz and find the gangs and Berto. He's going to want Beth on his turf."

"Jack, are you sure? You could be wrong," Mason said.

"I'm not wrong." Jack felt it down to his bones.

"Fine, we'll work the Pacific coast," Lydia said.

"I can get you on flights in two hours," Mason said.

Jack turned to Aiden. "You good with this?"

"I've got you covered, Jack."

He wished he could breathe easier, knowing he was getting support from every angle. But the knot in his gut got bigger with every minute Beth was out of his sight. What was she going through? What was happening to her at that very second?

Chapter Sixteen

She'd woken up hours ago? Minutes ago? She just didn't know. At least, she was used to the smell now, and it wasn't making her gag—much. To try to minimize the pain in her head she'd bent her knees, and rested her good cheek against her folded arms.

She gave a slight wiggle, she had to pee, but she'd be damned if she'd check out whatever smelly bucket there was looming about in the darkness. The truck hit another bump in the road, and Beth gritted her teeth. One more of those, and she might end up having an accident. As the truck finally slowed, she sighed in relief, but then she got scared. Really scared. What was going to happen?

Wait a damn minute. She was not going to be led like a lamb to slaughter. For almost a year she regretted taking off her clothes at the shack in the jungle. This time, she was going to go down fighting, no matter the consequences. The truck came to a stop. She pushed herself up and leaned against the wall, waiting to hear which way the container would open.

It was to her right. She heard something clank and stumbled towards the sound. The door opened and she squinted. Thank God it was night, so she wasn't blinded by the sun. She jumped down and fell flat, but she got maybe three feet when somebody grabbed her around the waist and held her up high. They squeezed her so tight her ribs hurt.

Beth screamed for help, the pain made the sounds shrill.

"Scream louder bitch, I love that sound, makes me hard." The scary phrase made her scream louder, and the man squeezed her even tighter.

"Stop it! This one's special to the boss."

Her elbow hit gravel as she was dropped to the ground.

"She stinks anyway." She looked up and saw two figures silhouetted against the moonlight. They looked huge.

"We're supposed to make sure she gets to the boss in good shape, so back the fuck off."

Good shape? That sounded promising.

"I need a bathroom."

"You need a bath."

"Fine, let me have a bath."

"Does this look like a hotel?" The man waved his hand. Beth looked around and saw train tracks and shipping containers. Then she saw something that looked like an oasis in a desert. It was a blue port-a-potty.

"Please, can I use the bathroom?"

"You mean the honey pot?" The man who had thrown her on the grown asked.

"Yes."

"What will you do for me?"

"Shut up, Bruce. Yeah, go on over there. We'll be watching you. Don't try anything stupid."

Beth ran to the blue structure. She was desperate for relief. It stank too, but she was passed caring. When she was done, she peeked outside and both men were looking her way. She went back to them. She'd try to escape when she had better odds.

"Now stay here," one of them said, pointing beside them. "We have more product coming, and then you're going to take a little trip."

Beth eyed the containers on the train and realized what was coming next. What she couldn't figure out was why they were waiting here. Shouldn't they be near the coast?

The wind started to blow and her damp clothes clung to her skin. Beth started to shiver.

"Give her your coat," the man in charge said.

"What?"

"I said give her your coat, Bruce."

"No."

"Bruce, give her your fucking coat. We can't afford for her to catch a fucking cold."

"I'm not giving her my coat." He buttoned it up and then patted his chest.

Beth watched in horror as the first man pulled out his knife and casually stabbed the second man in his hand. He screamed in pain.

"Shut up, Bruce, it didn't even go all the way through. Now give her your coat." Bruce stared at his bleeding hand.

"Don't make me kill you and pull it off your dead body. Give her the fucking coat." The first man didn't even raise his voice. Bruce fumbled with the buttons, shrugged it off, and threw it at her. Beth held the bloody coat away from her.

"Put it on." She looked at the man as he stared at her, and put on the coat.

Bruce was whimpering. She heard the sound of a truck and looked up.

"The shipment has arrived. You'll be taking a long trip, little lady. Hope you enjoyed your time in the honey pot." The first man laughed at his joke.

****

A damn skateboard park to get information should have been Jack's first clue he was dealing with a kid.

Aiden showed his cousin the picture of the gang tattoo on the dead man's hand.

"Can I see his face? It's a long shot, but I might know him," Alejandro said.

Aiden and Jack looked at one another.

"Look, I know the score. Just show me." Jack hated this. Alejandro was only fifteen, but his father assured both men he could handle himself and he would be the best member of the family to provide information about the gangs in Veracruz.

Jack scrolled through his phone and pulled up the video Rylie forwarded to them.

Alejandro's jaw tightened, but it was the only outward sign he was bothered by the sight of a man's tongue being cut out.

"I don't know the victim or the man who's doing the cutting. But look at the markings on the blade of the knife. Do you see how it's engraved? Can you zoom in on that?"

"It looks like teardrops," Aiden said.

"Those are drops of blood. It's for the *Hacha Sangrieta* gang. 'Bloody Ax' gang. Let me guess, they beheaded the poor guy with an ax."

Jack nodded.

"Well anyway, the number of blood drops on the blade tells you how high up in the organization you are. He's high up. I'd say he would be one of the top four or five."

Which made sense if Berto was actually in the room with him.

"We knew it was the *Hacha* gang because of the ax used for the beheading, but we didn't know about the blood drop engravings on the knives," Jack said.

"Most people don't. The *Hacha's* didn't have this kind of organization until last year. Until then, they were an unorganized street gang, but then they became more militarized."

"Do you know what happened?"

"There's a rumor one of the other gangs from Mexico City came in and took it over. They brought in the military too."

"Mercenaries," Aiden corrected.

"What?" Alejandro asked.

"Sounds like some of the mercs we've run into who are available to the highest bidder, and they don't care who they work for so long as the money is right," Jack spat out.

"They wear uniforms, and they say they have the backing of the government. Everybody is afraid of them. They're afraid they'll either be thrown in prison, or will end up butchered like the man in the video."

"Do you know where we can find these men?"

Alejandro looked at his cousin. "Aiden, this is serious shit. I know you're a SEAL, but there are just two of you. It's not like you have a bunch of men to take these guys down."

"Alejandro, you have a good point. I know how dangerous these men and this situation is. I don't enter it lightly, and your information will help us to stay safe."

"I could go with you. I have friends who could help too."

"I need you to stay here and continue to ask questions and provide us with intel. It's critical we have as much current information as possible. It will

247

help us stay safe. Can you and your friends do that for us?"

Jack saw how important Alejandro felt with his assignment, and was impressed once again by his Senior Chief's ability to mentor young recruits.

"I can. My father told me you wouldn't let me go," Alejandro said ruefully. "He said you could handle this all by yourself, but with one other SEAL you'd be able to kill *El Cuchilla* himself." 'The Blade', how fitting. Jack was sure it was what Berto was now calling himself.

They sat a moment longer watching some of the kids do tricks on their skateboards, and then Alejandro picked up his skateboard to join them.

****

They took a prop plane from the Peninsula over to Veracruz. If Jack could have found something humorous in anything, he would have found it funny Aiden was white knuckling it.

"Senior Chief, I never knew you were afraid of flying."

"This pilot is doing a shitty job. It's all I can do to keep from going up front and commandeering the stick from the asshole."

Jack thought about the take-off and admitted Aiden was right.

"We'll land in fifteen minutes."

"Most crashes happen on landings," Aiden muttered.

"I've never seen you like this before."

"That's because we've always had competent pilots. Let's go over our plan again."

"Another Canul is meeting us at the airport. Just how big is your family?"

"The O'Malley's were slackers compared to my mother's side of the family." Aiden grinned. "The Canuls are all over the place. This is a cousin once removed. He's old school."

"What does that mean?"

"You'll see."

****

"Uncle, this is my compatriot, Jack."

Jack felt like he was re-enacting a scene out of *The Godfather*. Leonard Canul was dressed in a three-piece white linen suit, and it accented his silver mustache and silver hair he'd brushed back from his face.

"Aiden. Come, I have your rooms ready at the *Emporio*. We shall eat lunch there and be seen."

"We have other things we need to do first." He felt naked without his gun and knife. Aiden's uncle gave him a knowing smile.

"It is the reason you have already been checked in. We will go to your room first. You will find in your room a wide variety of amenities from which you can choose."

"Uncle, you are still the man I remember." Aiden chuckled.

"You are not. I remember you having more sense, Nephew. This is a fool's errand."

Jack turned on the man. "We are not planning on taking down the operation. We want some information and intend to extract one woman. That is all."

"I know my nephew. He will be a fool."

Jack looked at Aiden and saw his uncomfortable expression.

"What am I missing?"

"Aiden has never been able to leave things undone. If he sees an injustice, he will insist on addressing everything. Are you telling me you are different than he is?"

Fuck!

They headed for the terminal exit. The man had a limousine waiting for them. Aiden was silent for the rest of the trip to the hotel. Leonard took them straight to their rooms. He pulled out three suitcases.

"What the hell? Are you selling weapons these days?"

"Bite your tongue. Your aunt would kill me if I went back to my old ways. I just own restaurants. But it doesn't mean I don't have my old contacts." The older man pulled out an AK47 from the largest suitcase. "I think this is too large for your needs, but having it when you are applying for a job as a mercenary will up your street credibility."

"Street cred," Jack corrected. He put it down and opened up the second largest suitcase. He made a sound of approval when he found a MK 12 SPR. It was the same rifle Griff used in Las Flores. "I'll take this. Where are the pistols?"

Leonard opened the last suitcase, it contained guns and knives.

"Do you see anything you like?"

Jack picked up a Sig Sauer P239.

"I thought you would like that. I brought plenty of ammunition for it." Aiden picked up the other one.

By the time they went down to the restaurant, Aiden and Jack were armed to the teeth. Jack felt like he was wearing his most comfortable pair of shoes.

They were halfway through lunch when the first man approached them.

"Leonard, who are your friends?"

Jack didn't like the guy. Not at all.

"Pietro, this is my nephew, Aiden Canul. This is his friend, Jack."

"Just Jack?"

"Yes." Jack glared at the man.

"I like last names."

"I only provide mine when I sign an employment contract."

Two more men walked up to the table, they heard Jack's comment and laughed as the first man got angry.

"Don't get your panties in a twist, Pietro. You know everyone here in Veracruz has a history. Do you blame the man for being cautious?"

Jack didn't like these men either. Something told him he wasn't going to like anyone until he got back to the states.

"So 'Just Jack' what do you do for a living?" one of the new men asked.

Jack threw his napkin down on the table and stood up to his full height, easily towering over all of the men.

"What the fuck do you think I do?"

"Sit down, Jack," Leonard said while Aiden stifled a laughed.

"I'm here to make some coin. Now if I wanted to put up with this kind of shit, I would have joined Match.com." This time, Aiden laughed out loud.

"Good luck with your asshole friend, Leonard." Pietro stalked away. The two other men stayed with smirks on their faces, assessing Jack.

"What?" Jack asked belligerently.

"Can you back up all this attitude?"

"I was an Army Ranger, what do you think?"

"I think they probably kicked you out. I think you had a problem with authority," the thinner of the two men said.

Jack looked over at Leonard. "Do I need to take this shit?"

"You do if you want a job. These men represent *El Cuchilla*. As a matter of fact, even if you don't want a job, I strongly suggest you show them some respect." Leonard leaned back in his chair.

"Fine, you're respected." Jack nodded his head. There was quiet, the thin man started to chuckle, and then he threw back his head and laughed. The other man took his lead and joined him.

"Oh Leonard, this man is funny. If he is as capable as he is humorous, then we could use him in our organization. This other man, he looks like you." He indicated Aiden. Jack looked at the two of them and realized there was a bit of a family resemblance.

"He's my nephew once removed."

"He, of course, is hired."

"Of course."

"If I may be so bold," Aiden spoke for the first time. "'Just Jack' and I were in the same unit. He's good. Not as good as me. But damn good."

"Sold. When can you both start? We have some work that needs to be done tomorrow."

"We got in today. Tomorrow would be a good day to start," Jack said.

"We'll pick you up, JJ."

"JJ?"

"Just Jack."

As they walked away, Jack sat down at the table. "You played it perfectly. Your friend is very arrogant, Aiden."

"He has his moments."

****

"Fourteen thousand. You owe us fourteen thousand. If you think to short us, imagine how hard it will be to support your family when your cantina is burned to the ground."

This was the fourth business they had come to today. This one wouldn't end well, Jack could tell. He'd seen the pregnant woman peeking around the corner.

"I don't have the money. I will next week. Please, give me another seven days."

"No. You said the same thing last week."

"I am giving you six thousand more."

"That covers the interest." He'd been sent out to *collect* with a burly man who had a brain the size of a pea. The big man got out his knife and started to clean under his nails.

"I just don't know what to do."

255

"Give us some collateral, and we'll go away." Jack watched as the man gave a sigh of relief. He pulled off his watch and his wedding ring. Jack's partner laughed.

"I'm talking about something of value."

"If not this, then what."

"We want your wife." The bar owner's eyes widened in terror.

"No. I've given you everything I have. She's sick."

"I saw her walking around, she's not sick." No, Jack knew who was sick. Every stop they made just kept getting worse. Aiden hadn't come on this collection stop, he'd been sidetracked to go meet with the thin man and his uncle. It left Jack alone on this goatfuck.

"Her due date is next week."

"Perfect. You'll get her back next week when you pay. Get her out here." He pointed his knife at the bar owner's throat. After a small cry from the back room, a small woman who looked to be twelve months pregnant came waddling out to where they were standing.

"Please don't hurt my husband, I beg you."

"Come with us, bitch."

"No. I don't want to have to play nursemaid," Jack said. "She looks like she's about to pop. She's going to be too much of a problem." Jack curled his lip as he looked her up and down.

"She looks fine. Haven't you ever had pregnant tail? It's sweet," his fat partner said. Jack's lip curled further.

"Great, you're going to do something more to get her to pop sooner. No wonder they have you doing shake-downs in the shittiest part of town. You've got to be the stupidest motherfucker I've ever met."

The man lunged at Jack with his knife. Just the move Jack was hoping he'd make. Jack side-stepped him, and the burly man went off balance to his right. Jack kicked him in the side of his knee and he howled as he went to the floor. The last thing he needed was this fool mouthing off. Jack needed him to make a stupid move so he could kill him.

"So who did you blow to get to work for the *Hacha's* anyway? Or did your mother get you the job?"

"You asshole." He lunged upwards and pulled his gun out of his jacket. From the corner of his eye, Jack saw the couple duck behind the bar. He pulled out his gun and shot the man right between the eyes. Silence reigned.

"Mister, get out here." He was impressed how the man motioned his wife to stay down when she tried to stand up.

"This is on me. I'll explain how this was a conflict between the two of us, and you weren't at fault. But I need your cooperation. I need the six grand, the watch, your wedding ring, and your wife's rings." She had her palm up in a heartbeat, holding her rings. He approved of this woman, she understood what was important, and it wasn't some gold and diamonds.

Jack took the money, and jewelry, and stuffed it into his pocket. Then he bent and hefted the bulky man over his shoulder, and walked out into the afternoon sun to the car, and threw him into the trunk. Not one person gave him a second glance.

He and Aiden calculated it would be another eighteen hours before Beth would probably be in Veracruz if she were shipped by truck. Three days if she was shipped by train. Either way, he would have to spend his time worming his way into this sick organization so he could be part of the welcoming committee.

Chapter Seventeen

Three unconscious girls were dumped into the shipping container before the train began moving. At least this time, the holes were bigger so Beth could see her way around. There were blankets, and a makeshift toilet cut into the floor of the container so their waste would fall onto the tracks. It was these little considerations that made this seem like the Taj Mahal.

She'd checked each girl's pulse to make sure they were alive even before the door closed, causing the evil man to laugh.

"Don't worry girly, we wouldn't have killed such high-end product."

"I don't believe you." Beth knelt by the young blonde girl and touched her neck to feel for the heartbeat.

"I don't care if you believe me or not." He slammed the door shut, and she heard the clang of the lock. Long minutes later the train began to move. There were enough blankets to use some as pillows under the three girl's heads.

After what seemed like three or four hours, the first girl started to rouse. She didn't say anything. She didn't even really move, and it's when Beth realized she wasn't a new captive. She went over to her.

"My name is Beth. We're on a train by ourselves. None of the men are here with us." She was young. Too damn young to be on this train. She was a pretty American brunette. She didn't open her eyes.

"Can you hear me? My name is Beth. We're safe for now."

"How long have we been here?"

"They put us on this train about four hours ago."

"Are Irene and Missy here too?" She opened her eyes and looked around.

"I don't know. There are two other girls. What's your name?"

"I'm Joanne." She sat up, holding the blanket around her. Even in the dim light, Beth saw she was still just a teenager.

"How old are you?"

"I'm sixteen. How old are you?"

"I'm twenty-two."

"You didn't run away from home?" Joanne questioned.

"No. I was kidnapped. What happened to you?"

"Some guy saw me living on the street. I wasn't being a prostitute or anything, honest." Beth's heart went out to the girl the way she said 'honest.'

"Joanne, it wouldn't matter if you were."

"It wouldn't?"

"No, it wouldn't. Nobody deserves to be taken against their will."

"That's exactly what happened. A guy came up, and he offered to buy me a cheeseburger. I said I wouldn't go with him, so he brought it to me. He did it for three days straight, so I knew he was a good guy, ya know?"

"I would have thought he was a good guy too. What happened next?"

"He said I could crash at his place no strings attached." Her chin fell to her chest. "I was so stupid," she mumbled.

"No, you weren't. You just trusted someone who was a predator."

"How did you get caught?"

"I was kidnapped at gunpoint."

"Oh my God. Why are they doing this?"

261

Beth thought about how to answer the question. "Because they're bad people."

"We're so screwed. It was really bad with my folks, but I wish I were with them now."

"They're going to sell us aren't they?" A small voice came from behind her. Beth turned and saw the older blonde girl was awake.

"That's what they intend to do, yes. But we're going to come up with a plan to help ourselves."

"Can we do that?" Joanne asked.

"I have some friends who'll be looking for me, and I want to make it easy for them to find me. So it means I need to make it tough on these assholes to keep me."

"How do we do that?" the blonde girl asked.

"First we wait for the last girl to wake up, and then we start planning."

****

"He was dumb. Dumb deserves to die." Jack dumped the corpse at the feet of the thin man named Ruiz. He looked at the dead man, and then his beady eyes looked at Jack, assessing him.

"Tell me again what happened."

"No, I've already told you twice." Jack's mouth was dry, but he was damn near certain he was playing it right. This man appreciated strength, and Jack explaining himself over and over again showed weakness.

Finally, he laughed. "I always thought this man was an idiot too. I never expected it would be one of us who killed him."

"Be thankful it was, it made clean up easier." Ruiz laughed harder.

"I like you, JJ."

"Here's the money and the jewelry. I'll go collect next week. He won't disappoint me. He'll have figured out how to get the rest for us."

"I have no doubt." Ruiz bent down and pulled the watch off the wrist of the dead man and added it to the handful of jewelry. "Manuelo, come and get rid of this before a rat starts gnawing on it, will you?" He called to the man across the room.

Ruiz motioned for Jack to follow him up the stairs.

"Where's Aiden?"

"Since he's a known quantity, with familial references, we have him on...more delicate projects."

"Are they more lucrative?" Jack asked.

263

Ruiz got a calculating look in his eye as he glanced at Jack.

"You're still on trial, and killing your team mates is not really a great way to prove your worthiness."

"That's bullshit. I did you a favor. Go ahead and tell me you weren't planning on having him killed within the month. He was a detriment to your organization."

"Be that as it may, it was still my decision to make not yours. If you pull that kind of shit again, without my sanction, you could be the one dead. Am I making myself clear?"

Jack gave the man the deferential nod he so clearly expected. He couldn't wait to kill him as well, but first he had to find Beth.

"Aiden should be back soon. We have this other side of the business besides collecting support money from business owners."

"Drugs?"

"Again, JJ, you need to quit assuming you know everything. Take a few moments and allow me to explain things to you. I guess you want a fast payday, is that it?"

"I've noticed supplying muscle for the drug trade has made a lot of my friends a lot of money. So yeah, I'd like to cash in."

"What if I told you we have something even more lucrative? But it requires finesse? So far, you haven't shown much. I need to see patience, do you think you can stop making assumptions, and maybe not kill someone for twelve hours?" Ruiz smirked as he said the last part.

"I can't promise. If you send me out with someone who is going to blow our operation, I'm taking him down. Finesse is a fine thought, but it doesn't do you a damn bit of good if you're behind bars or six feet under."

"Point taken." Ruiz opened the door and ushered him into a room looking like something out of an old Western bordello. He looked around, there was a woman in a negligee seated on the divan, and she was counting money.

"Ruiz," she acknowledged and went back to counting.

"Hello, beauty. I have a new colleague I'd like you to meet."

"In a minute."

Ruiz motioned for Jack to sit in a wingback chair, and then he went to a fully stocked bar and poured two drinks from a decanter. He handed one to Jack.

265

"The finest *reposado* tequila from my grandfather's fields." He clinked his glass against Jack's and they drank.

"Done. So, you're JJ? I'm Helen." She swept the cash into a lock box. "Pour me some tequila, Ruiz." He got up from the other wingback chair and poured them all a round of tequila.

"You killed our resident dumbass today. Good for you. I like you. You're pretty as well." Ruiz flushed at the comment. Not good. She looked from one man to the other.

"Ruiz, if I feel like fucking JJ, it's my business. Hell, I might even want you to watch." Jack wished he could have another shot of tequila. He'd known the right way to play Ruiz was not to cower, but with Helen, any kind of back-talk could end up in a painful death.

"Oh my God, look at the pretty boy. He doesn't like the idea of us getting it on. What's going on? Do you have a girlfriend? A boyfriend? Tell mama." She held out her glass and Ruiz plucked it from her hand and refilled it. This time, she sipped her drink and eyed Jack over the rim of the shot glass.

"I expect an answer."

"I'm engaged."

"Are you in love?"

"Yes."

"Are you faithful?"

"Yes."

"Always?"

"Yes."

"Well okay then. You'll be perfect to work with our merchandise. But understand this now, JJ. If you are ever caught touching the girls in an inappropriate manner, you will be castrated. I normally would give you one warning, but since you're telling me you're faithful, I'm going to be especially harsh in your case."

"Merchandise?"

"Ruiz, didn't you tell him?"

"I didn't know if we wanted to use him."

"Hell, anyone who had the good sense to kill Duarte gets my vote. Of course we're going to use him." Who was she, and where was Berto? Oh, fuck it, who cares, if it got him what he wanted. He wanted Beth. He wanted her safe. He wanted her now.

"We haven't been properly introduced, Helen. My name is Jack, not JJ, I'm a former Army Ranger."

"Actually, you were dishonorably discharged, former Captain Richards. But if you insist, yes, let's do this

267

dance. I'm Helen Vasquez. My brother, God rest his soul, used to be in charge of these wayward boys here in Veracruz. I mentioned on numerous occasions that he and a bull in heat had the same level of organizational skills, but he never listened to me. When *El Cuchilla* came to town, my brother was gutted. *El Cuchilla* noticed I did have organizational skills, gave me a position, and now both of us are making a great deal of money."

Jack got the distinct impression Helen had something to do with her brother's gutting.

"Your friend Aiden has already been introduced to the organization. Of course, his uncle has run back to hide behind the skirts of his wife. It's amazing to me how people can change, and not for the better. Leonard was once someone to be reckoned with, to be respected. Now he is weak because of a woman." She took another sip.

"Tell me, does your woman make you weak?"

"No, she makes me strong." Then he figured out how to play her. "Any man who was lucky enough to stand by your side would only be stronger for it." She preened.

"This is so. But he would have to be the right man. Since you're taken, perhaps Aiden?" Her voice trailed off and she gave Ruiz a significant look.

What kind of sick game was she playing with this poor bastard?

"So tell me about the merchandise? Asia? Russia? The Ukraine? Local?"

"All of the above, and some from the United States."

"Very impressive. I would have thought taking girls from the US would have painted a target on your back."

"There is a large population of runaway and forgotten girls, and young women. It's easy. We just scoop them up."

"Why take the risk? If your client wants Caucasians, why not stick with the Russians?"

"Because the Middle Eastern clientele especially want the prestige of having Americans. We believe in providing the client with what they want." The tequila was not settling well.

"Okay, makes sense. So what's my part? And better yet, how will I be compensated?"

Helen laughed. "I love a no-nonsense man. Is Aiden to the point like you are?"

"Even more so. Comparatively speaking, I'm evasive." He could feel the waves of animosity pouring off Ruiz. The man pulled out a knife and twirled it between his fingers.

"Oh quit playing with your knife. Yes, I know you're one of *El Cuchilla's* favorites. But so am I."

"You best remember it. I don't think he would want his girlfriend playing with the hired help."

"I'm not the one he wants, remember?" They gave each other a significant look.

"Tell me about *El Cuchilla*, am I going to be meeting him?" Jack took a surreptitious look at the knife Ruiz was playing with and saw even more drops of blood than the one the man in the video used. It looked like he was dealing with Berto's right-hand people.

"If you prove yourself to be useful you will," Ruiz said. "And if you don't rock the boat." He glanced at him meaningfully. Jack understood what it meant. Stay the fuck away from Helen. It would not be a problem.

"I won't rock the boat. You tell me how to be useful and I'll do it."

"You'll get more details tonight. We're going out to dinner. It'll be fun. You'll get to meet more members of our little family." Helen purred. Ruiz looked at him, as he used his knife to clean his nails. Everybody had clean nails in this organization.

****

All of the girls were awake. They'd been on the train for over a day and a half. It was when she was using the airy facility Beth had her epiphany. There were two pieces of wood to act as a makeshift seat. They basically had an escape hatch cut into the floor.

"Get me blankets," she called to the girls.

"What's wrong?" Joanne asked as she brought over the blankets.

"Nothing. I think something is actually right."

The train made four stops since they'd been on it. On their next stop, maybe they'd have an opportunity to get the hell off. In the dim light, Beth examined the makeshift toilet. There was no way they could fit with the wood in place. She took one of the blankets and cleaned the opening. She put her head through to see how wide the hole was in the floor of the container.

"Joanne, it's wide enough for us to fit through if we can pull up the wood." The other two girls came over to see what the commotion was about.

"Look what Beth found. We could climb out the hole," Joanne exclaimed.

"While the train is moving?"

"No, dummy, when the train is stopped," Joanne snapped.

"I can't fit through there," Irene said.

"Of course you can't," Joanne said derisively. "Beth is going to make it bigger."

"Girls, we have to work together." Beth kept her voice calm and positive.

"How do we make the hole bigger?" Missy asked.

"See these pieces of wood?"

"I can't see anything, it's too dark," Irene complained.

"You can see to piss, can't you?" Joanne jumped down her throat.

"Come closer, Irene. Put your hand here, do you feel how the wood is bolted to the floor?"

"How are we going to get the wood out of the way so we can get through the hole if it's bolted to the floor?" Missy asked. It was a good question. One Beth hadn't figured out yet. The bolts were on so tight it would take a wrench to get them off. But the wood wasn't very thick.

"We're going to have to break the wood, and then pull it away from the hole." She was met by silence. She didn't blame them.

"Who has the strongest shoes?"

"What?"

"Let me see your shoes. We're going to have to kick the wood. I want to see who has the best shoes to kick the wood." Unfortunately, Beth was wearing ballet flats, so it wasn't going to help much. She'd be pulling the broken pieces of wood away from the hole.

"Me." Joanne held up her foot, and everybody looked at her combat boot.

"We have a winner!" Beth grinned, and all the girls laughed. Thank God, because she needed them to be in the right frame of mind. This wasn't going to be easy.

"Beth, I should kick near the edges, right?"

"Yep. But we're going to be on either side of you, and you're going to hold onto our shoulders." It took a lot longer than Beth hoped to start getting the boards to loosen. Joanne was breathing hard, and her kicks were getting much weaker before the first crack sounded.

"You can stop now."

"No, I want to kick it out."

"That was never the plan, Joanne. We just needed you to loosen the wood so I can pull. You've done your part, now let me." Joanne sat against the wall with Missy and Irene. Beth started to pry the wood. After twenty minutes her muscles were aching.

Three different times her hands slipped and she got splinters, and the last time wood sliced into her palm making her gasp in pain.

"Are you all right?" Missy called out.

"I'm fine."

"Do you need help?"

"I've almost got it." And she did, but now she had to figure out how to stop the bleeding. Beth took one of the blankets and tore it, and then wrapped it around her hand. When she saw how it protected her hand, she did it for the other one as well. She should have thought to do this much earlier.

A hand touched her shoulder and she jerked.

"I'm not tired anymore. Can I help?"

"Sure, Joanne. Wrap your hands in the blankets, and then let's finish pulling up the wood."

Together they finished the job. They looked through the hole and watched the train tracks as they sped by. Now they just had to wait for the next stop. Beth hoped it would be someplace they could get help.

Chapter Eighteen

"Mason, I'll know for sure tonight, but I'm pretty sure it's all going down here. I definitely know they're bringing American girls."

"That jives with what Melvin said about the runaways. We didn't think they would be going out on the Gulf side."

"Apparently they're a hit in the Middle Eastern market."

"That's sick." It was Drake. Jack realized he was on speaker.

"So you're going to call us back tonight?" Mason asked.

"Yep. Aiden and I are going out for a fancy dinner."

"Okay, call us back." The line went dead.

Jack looked around the hotel room. He was still waiting for Aiden. Dinner was in an hour. Helen told him to dress up. It was all surreal. Leonard must have expected the dress-up part of the events because

275

he'd provided dress clothes along with all the weapons. It was another layer of creepy if you asked him.

Jack heard the key card and was up with a gun before the door could open. Aiden entered with his hands up.

"Hey partner, nice of you to finally show up," Jack said as he lowered his gun.

"I'm not sure I want to be your partner. I hear they end up dead."

"Only the stupid ones."

Aiden headed towards his bedroom and Jack followed him. He pulled off his shirt. Jack saw the blood on it.

"Yours?" he asked.

"No." He scowled. "I was involved in an interrogation. This one was just a beating. Fucker deserved it. He was a child molester. I would have gladly helped, but I was only in the spray zone."

"Nice first day on the job."

"Again, I didn't kill anybody, so I'd say mine was a step up."

Jack thought about when he pulled the trigger, and he didn't feel any regret. What did that make him?

"I called Mason, and put him on alert he'd probably be moving this way."

"You got intel on the slave trade? On Beth?"

"Definitely on human trafficking, including Americans. We'll hear more tonight."

"I need a shower."

"So do I. I'll see you in the living room in twenty."

Jack hit the shower. He didn't know what made him feel more unclean—the killing or Helen. As he dressed, he realized he needed to warn Aiden about his admirer. For just a moment he considered not telling him after everything that had gone on wasn't he entitled to a little entertainment?

He went into the room connecting the two bedrooms and Aiden was waiting for him. He'd found the beer and offered him one.

"Well since you gave me a beer I suppose I better tell you about Helen."

"Who's Helen?"

"Your soon-to-be fiancé."

"Ah fuck, now what?"

"There's this psycho bitch. I swear she'd eat her own young. When I told her I was engaged, she set her sights on you."

"Thanks," Aiden said sarcastically. "I take it she's going to be at dinner tonight?"

"She's going to be the hostess."

"Uncle didn't mention her."

"Your uncle has the good sense to cut and run." There was a knock on the door and both men drew their guns. Jack opened the door and let in Ruiz.

"Is all this necessary?" Ruiz asked, indicating the guns.

"We like to be careful, you never know if it's a friend or an enemy who might be coming to visit," Aiden said.

"And we still don't." Jack put away his gun.

"No, you don't. Can you offer me a drink?" Ruiz asked.

"Tequila?" Jack headed towards the bar.

"*Reposado*." Ruiz pointed to the bottle he wanted. Jack poured him a glass.

"None for you?"

"I'll drink tonight. Tell me what to expect," Jack demanded.

278

"Well, JJ," Ruiz said after his first sip. "There will be many men who are not going to be happy you took it upon yourself to kill Duarte."

"Fuck 'em."

"Hey JJ, you might want to mellow the hell out," Aiden yelled from the couch where he was dinking with his cuff links.

"Ruiz, doesn't Aiden look nice?" Jack asked. "What do you think Helen will say when she sees him?"

Aiden glared at him.

"Enough of this bullshit. We need to go."

****

The train finally started to slow down.

"Remember what I told you. I'm going to go first. The stops last for *at least* five minutes. If someone has to get caught and get in trouble, let it be me."

"I want out of here, I want to go first," Irene whined.

"Shhhh, she's doing us a favor by going first." Joanne waved her hand at the girl.

The train stopped. There were blankets lining the hole so they wouldn't get chewed up with splinters. Beth leaned down as far as she could with Joanne holding her feet.

279

"I don't see anyone." She motioned for Joanne to help her up.

"Okay, I'm going to go." It was just getting dark outside—perfect for their purposes. It was light enough for them to see, but soon they'd be camouflaged by darkness. She dropped lightly to the ground and tried to make as little noise as possible. She ducked as she got out from under the train, but still managed to hit her head against a low hanging piece of metal. It snagged her hair, and she struggled to untangle it so she could get free.

She pressed against the side of the train and looked around. There was another one beside her. Perfect! Nobody would see the four of them. But what was on the side of the other train? This time, she crawled under the next train.

There was a small dilapidated terra cotta stucco depot. Empty. Why had they stopped if nobody was around? She didn't want to have the girls leave the train car until she had the answer, but she also didn't want the train to start moving either. She rushed back to get them. Joanne's head was sticking out when she returned.

"Is it safe? Can we go?"

"Have the others get the remaining bottles of water. Hand them to me, and then we're all going. Tell them to be quiet."

They handed her eleven bottles of water.

"Give me a blanket so I can carry them. Wait, give me all the blankets," Beth instructed.

She helped steady each girl as they came out. Soon they were all standing in front of her. She made makeshift backpacks with the blankets and the water and tied them to each girl.

"We're going to crawl under the trains so you don't hit your heads like I did." She gave a rueful laugh, and the girls grinned. She was trying to make it seem like an adventure, and Missy seemed less scared.

"Okay, let's go. So far I haven't seen anyone. Follow me closely, and don't talk."

As soon as they were under the second train their train began to move. Beth said a prayer of thanks they'd made it in time. It also told her they had to move fast. She needed to think fast. How was she going to play this?

As soon as they were standing next to the second train and looking at the deserted depot, she decided to brazen it out.

"Follow me. I'll do the talking since I'm a native."

"And you can speak Spanish," Joanne said out of the corner of her mouth. Beth bit back a laugh. The girl had a point.

They walked the three steps to the door, and Beth looked at the train schedule and map posted. It said they were nine stops away from Veracruz. They were halfway between Mexico City and Veracruz. God, she needed help.

Beth grinned. She just helped herself, and these girls. Now she had to keep doing it. Opening the door, she saw an old woman with a toddler sitting on a concrete bench. To the left the ticket window had bars and a closed signed. Beth signaled for the three girls to go sit at the back of the room so they wouldn't draw attention.

"Pardon, *Senora*, but when are they going to be selling tickets?"

"They should still be open," came her resigned reply. The little boy looked at Beth, his brown eyes big with delight. "They set their own hours. I will wait and hope." She looked over her shoulder at the girls.

"Are you in trouble?"

Beth didn't respond.

"This is a bad place to be if you're in trouble. It is why I'm buying a ticket for my daughter and grandson to go my brother in Quintana Roo."

"You are a good mother." The little boy lifted his arms to Beth and said, "up." She laughed.

"Yes, little man, I'll pick you up." Beth hefted him into her arms and winced. Her hand was really beginning to hurt. He patted her face.

"Boo-boo."

"Yes, I banged my face."

"I think you're in trouble. I think those white girls are in trouble too. You shouldn't be here when the man who sells the tickets gets here. We'll leave."

"*Senora*, I don't want you to get into any trouble," Beth protested.

"The day I turn my back on other women in need is the day they can put me in the ground." She turned to Joanne and the other girls. "Tell them to come with us." The old woman picked up her huge purse, and Beth continued to hold the cute little boy.

"Joanne, Missy, and Irene let's go."

Chapter Nineteen

"Call them, I've got to go take another shower."
Aiden threw his suit coat across the room. Even from
here, Jack could smell Helen's perfume.

Jack pulled out his phone.

"You're on speaker."

"The shipment from Tijuana will arrive tomorrow.
There is product coming in from overseas in the port.
They talked about it like they would be culling cattle
tomorrow night."

He was met by dead silence.

"Did I lose you?"

"No," Mason said quietly. "We're just absorbing it,
Jack. We'll be there. Do you have any idea how
many people are in their operation? Or how many
people will need to be rescued besides Beth?"

"I met the dream team we'd be up against."

"Jack, give them the truth." He turned and looked at
Aiden, who was standing there with a towel wrapped
around his hips. He put his phone on speaker.

"Mason, this is Aiden. Jack's right, some of these guys are absolute idiots, but they are stone cold killers. They'll butcher each other to get to you. Also, they won't care if the women live or die. These are the original gang members Berto gathered together, the original *Hacha Sangrientas*."

"How many are there?" Clint asked.

"Probably about fifteen tomorrow night. Plus, there are going to be five of Berto's mercs, two of which are us." Aiden grinned.

"We still haven't had the pleasure of meeting Berto," Jack said. He'd really been hoping he'd be at the dinner tonight. But apparently he had other plans. Jack was assured he'd be there to open the container from Tijuana.

"We're going to have to really coordinate things. The train Beth is on is coming in four hours before the boat with the three containers from overseas," Aiden said.

"I've been thinking," Jack said. "What if we do an old fashioned train robbery before the train reaches Veracruz. Get Beth safely off the train before it reaches here?" He saw Aiden's face light up with a smile.

"Son, that's brilliant. I love the simple plans."

"Melvin was positive she'd be coming on a truck, but if you know it's a train, he should be able to track it." Jack grimaced at the bad pun Clint made. Hopefully, it hadn't been on purpose.

"If we fly into Mexico City, she should be just about there or a little past it on the way to Veracruz."

Jack itched to be in on Beth's rescue, but what they said made sense.

"Jack?" Aiden was staring at him.

"Mason, I agree. In the meantime, we'll work on getting all the intel we can on this. Are you going to bring in other agencies?"

"We will on the ship in Veracruz, no on Beth." Jack sighed in relief. He only wanted his fellow SEALs working to get Beth home safely.

"How are you holding up, Jack?" Drake asked.

Jack swallowed, he could only think about Beth and what she must be going through.

"He's doing good. He's only killed one man so far for being stupid," Aiden answered.

"No shit?" Drake asked.

"It's true," Aiden confirmed.

"Leave some for us," Drake said.

"Will do," Jack said. "How're you going to be able to find the train Beth is on?"

"We're going to coordinate train schedules, and ultimately get some satellite photos," Clint explained.

"In other words, don't ask." Drake laughed.

There was a knock on the door.

"We've got to shut this down, fellas." Jack pressed end. Aiden somehow had a gun in his hand, which Jack found amazing since he was only wearing a towel. Jack pulled his and went to the door. It was Helen.

"Aiden, you didn't need to get all dressed up for me," she purred.

"To what do we owe this honor?"

"Ruiz is worried about your loyalty. We're going to have you meet our employer for breakfast tomorrow. He'll decide if you are going to work with us on our endeavors tomorrow night."

Aiden and Jack looked at one another.

"And you Helen? Are you worried?" Aiden asked.

"I'm not the one who is jealous." She meandered over to Aiden, who still had his gun in his hand. She ran her nails over his ripped abdomen and looked at his towel in disappointment after seeing how there was no reaction.

"So I don't do it for you, huh? Are you taken like this one is?"

"No, I'm not taken, but my thoughts are elsewhere."

"I'm really getting sick of the good ones being enamored with different women. Or is it a woman?"

"It's a woman," he confirmed.

"Is she pretty?"

"Inside and out. She's a doctor." Jack winced. Did Aiden really have to throw down that way with the psycho bitch?

"Well, I'll tell you the same thing I told your 'not so little' friend. Don't touch the merchandise. If you do, I'll have you castrated."

"Good to know, I've always wanted to avoid castration." She barked out a laugh.

"Well, gentlemen, be ready to be picked up for breakfast at seven a.m. I won't be there, it will just be *El Cuchilla* and Ruiz. I don't believe in mornings."

"As for our other partner, he'll be flying in next week. You'll meet him then."

What other partner?

"What other partner," Aiden asked.

"We get our product from the East. We have to have a supply side and a distribution side. We're the distribution side. However, the supply side has had more opinions over here. As a matter of fact, he wants to do more on the American and Canadian coasts. *El Cuchilla* is interested in hearing him out."

"Why are we so lucky to meet him?" Aiden asked.

"According to my intel, you speak Chinese. Both Cantonese and Mandarin. This is very beneficial. And JJ is the kind of pretty blonde he likes to look at. Our supplier...he likes pretty."

They watched her leave.

****

"Mama, what were you thinking? These girls are obviously criminals. If they find them here, we could end up in prison." Beth didn't like the older woman's daughter. It was funny because it seemed like her son didn't like her either. He kept holding out his arms to Beth and trying to wiggle out of his mother's arms.

"Stop it, Juan. She can't hold you."

"Margarita, they are staying with me. This is my house. You and Juan are leaving tomorrow as soon as I can buy you tickets."

"Good." She left the room and slammed the door to her small bedroom.

"I apologize. She is spoiled."

"She's a bitch," Joanne said. The woman gave Joanne a narrow-eyed look, and Beth sighed. 'Bitch' was a word easily understood by most Mexicans.

"Joanne, back off, you don't know what she was saying."

"Sure I do. I might not understand Spanish, but she was definitely telling her mom we were bad news and to get rid of us. Do we have to go?"

"No, we don't. At least, I don't think we do. Can you take the girls back to the room Senora Lomas gave us? I think the more out of sight we are, the better."

"What about you?"

"I'm going to help her with dinner, and try to see about finding a phone to use."

"You have people you can call?" Joanne sounded hopeful.

"Boy, do I."

"Gee, Beth, it would be great if someone would come and help us. Are you sure they would?"

"I'm positive." Beth walked over and hugged the young girl. She whispered in her ear, "My boyfriend is a Navy SEAL."

"For real?" she squealed.

"For real."

"But we don't even know where we are, how can he find us?"

"If anyone can, Jack can. Now take the others and go into the back, okay?" Joanne grinned and gathered the other two girls.

Beth turned and saw Senora Lomas looking at her.

"You are good with those girls. How did you come to be traveling together?"

"We've all been kidnapped. We were going to be sold." The woman didn't look surprised.

"It is sad. I have seen many bad things in my life. It can be very bad for women. How did you escape?" Beth explained about the train and the hole in the floor. Senora Lomas' eyes got very wide, and then she insisted on looking at Beth's hand.

"Here, let me get some ointment. It looks very painful." It was, but Beth didn't want to complain. A little bit of pain was a small price to pay for their freedom.

"Do you have a phone I can use?"

"I don't, and my daughter will not let you use hers. Do you need to make a call outside of Mexico?"

Dammit. Beth hadn't thought of that, but she did. She couldn't imagine anybody's calling plan supporting an international call. How did you even go about making a collect call anymore?

"Senora Lomas, do you know how to make a collect call to America?"

"No, but I'm sure little Jorge next door will know. He watches all of the American programs on the TV. The little boy knows everything. We will go and ask to use his mother's phone."

They plodded through the muddy walkway between the two little homes and a very large woman opened the door.

"Flora, what orphan have you dragged home this week?"

"This is Beth. It's a long story. Are you going to invite us in Lupita?" The big woman laughed, and stepped back to allow them entry into her house. Behind her was a small boy holding a handheld video game.

"Ah, just the young man we're looking for. Jorge, this is my friend Beth. She needs your help."

"Are you on the run?"

"Jorge, what made you ask that question?" his mother admonished.

"I saw her come in with her three white friends. They look like criminals, and they were sneaking in with Senora Lomas. Are the police after you?"

"I'm going to take away your TV privileges for a week if you're not more respectful Jorge Lodge. Are we clear?" His mother's voice boomed through the house, and the boy shrugged his shoulders.

"You'll just let me watch it tomorrow anyway. But I'll be nice, I don't want to hurt her feelings. But are you a criminal?"

Beth sighed. "No, I'm not a criminal. Criminals are after me. I need your help to get away from them. I have people who will come and save me if I can get ahold of them. Otherwise, I need to find a way to leave before the criminals come and find us."

"Our police here are very bad. They are criminals too," Jorge said.

The women looked at one another.

"It's sad when even one so young knows how corrupt our system is. How can we help you?"

"I need a telephone, and to make a collect call to California."

All three women looked at the little boy.

"That is simple."

"Thank, God," Senora Lomas said. Lupita fished a phone out of the pocket of the hoodie she wore and handed it to her son. Jorge pushed in many numbers and then shoved the phone to Beth.

"Talk to the operator." He grinned proudly.

"Hello? I need to make a collect call to Jack Preston, let me give you his number."

****

"Do you need to get that?" Berto asked.

Jack ignored the phone in his pocket. It was on a very low vibrate, but Berto was watching him like a hawk.

"It's nobody."

"I insist. You're my guest. You're also my employee, I'm interested in what goes on in my employee's lives."

Jack pulled out the phone.

"I don't recognize the number. If it isn't somebody I know, I have a policy of not answering." He put the phone back in his pocket.

"You should be more careful who you give your number to," Berto said.

"Yes I should, that's good advice." Jack forked another slice of mango and chewed. Berto focused his attention on Aiden.

"Ruiz and Helen were telling me about your Uncle Leonard. He sounds like an interesting man. It's too bad he is not someone we can talk into working with us."

"He's been reformed by love."

"A woman should never lead a man around by his cock. The man is in charge. You will meet my woman tonight. She will know who is in charge from the very second she lays eyes on me. It will be a very satisfying reunion."

Jack put his fork down.

"You stopped eating. Don't you agree, JJ?"

"It depends on the woman, *El Cuchilla*. Some women need to be put in their place," he said thinking of Helen. "Some women need to be loved and cared for."

"Ruiz said you have a woman."

"I do."

"You believe in loving and caring, I suppose."

"I do."

295

"Let me give you some advice. First you make sure she knows who's in charge. What about you Aiden, do you have a woman?"

"I have one in mind, yes."

"How do you plan to treat her?"

"Whatever way will win her."

Berto laughed. "You're a man after my own heart. Don't forget, some women like the back of your hand. Don't be afraid to use it."

Aiden didn't show any outward sign of disgust, but Jack knew his friend. He was going to need another shower.

"So you are both Army Rangers? But only you were dishonorably discharged. It was for what? The details were sparse."

"My captain and I had a disagreement over a woman. He thought I was being too harsh with her."

"I'm confused; you must explain this to me."

"This was before I met my love. I didn't always believe in love and caring. So, Berto, I can understand your ways of treating women. As I said, it depends on the woman."

Berto slammed the butt of his fork down on the table, causing the plates to clatter.

"I like you, JJ! You will be good for our organization.
I will have you meet the train with *mi amor* tonight."
He grinned broadly. Jack grinned in return.
Everything was going perfectly until he and Aiden got
back to the room and he heard his message.

"Jack, this is Beth. I'm with three other girls. We're
in a town called Rallos. I don't know how safe it is, or
how long we can stay here with Senora Lomas
without causing problems for her. Here is the phone
number of her neighbor. Please call us. I'm going to
try Lydia next. I love you."

He called the number and got voicemail.

"Goddamit!" he roared.

****

"Lydia!"

"Beth, is this really you?"

"Oh Lydia, you're safe. I was so worried."

"Are you shitting me? Jesus Beth, you had a gun to
your head. They hit you and drove you away. I
thought you were on a train to Veracruz."

"How did you know?" Beth looked up and saw the
two women were staring at her. "Never mind. I need
help. I can't go to the authorities. The ladies I'm

297

with are telling me they can't be trusted. I'm in a little town called Rallos."

"Hold on, the guys just landed in Mexico City about an hour ago. They planned to rescue you from the train. You just made their job a whole hell of a lot easier, little sister." Beth was warmed by the pride she heard in Lydia's voice.

There was silence on the phone.

"Beth?"

"Is that you, Mason?"

"Can you tell us exactly where you are? Clint is getting GPS coordinates. You're on speaker phone." There was a lot of background noise, and she was having trouble hearing him.

"If you asked where I am, I'm in a city called Rallos." She looked at Lupita.

"What's your address?"

"Give them mine," Senora Lamos said. "5 Via Fleur."

"I'm at 5 Via Fleur. I have three other girls with me."

"Clint said we should be there in an hour and a half. Stay put Beth. Just hunker down, we'll be there."

"Who were you talking to?" Beth spun around. There were three men in uniforms in the doorway. Behind her was Senora Lomas' daughter.

"What do you want? This is my house, get out!" Lupita's voice was loud in the small kitchen.

"You are harboring a fugitive. Hand over the phone." The man in the uniform held out his hand. Senora Lomas was furious. Jorge peered up at the adults, his eyes huge.

"You did this, you called them didn't you?" Senora Lomas raged at her daughter.

"I told you they were criminals. We shouldn't be involved." Beth winced as they grabbed her upper arm and she was pulled out of the house. There was a jeep and a flat-bed truck waiting out front. Joanne, Missy, and Irene were sitting dejectedly in the back of the truck with two men and automatic rifles. Missy and Irene were crying.

"Get in." The man pushed her towards the tailgate. Beth struggled, and he shoved her, once again her face met steel and she saw stars. The next thing she knew she had her head in Joanne's lap.

"Your head isn't that hard, would you quit trying to crack it open, Beth?" she whispered.

"Okay." How were Mason and the team going to find them now?

Chapter Twenty

"Jack, you have to get it together," Aiden said.

"I don't think I can." They were positioned at the far end of the pier. It was five hours since watching Berto go bat shit crazy when the train arrived and the shipping container was empty.

They both watched as the huge crane lowered another container off the ship. The *Hacha's* weren't let on the boat this time, which was another deviation from the norm. Today was not Berto's day. Ruiz was shitting bricks. So they were all waiting for three red containers, each with a black 'X', to come ashore.

"Is that one of them?" Aiden said pointing?

"Yep."

"Where the fuck is DHS and DEA? Hell, I'd be happy with the Mexican authorities."

"I spoke to Lydia an hour ago. She told me they were coordinating a takedown."

"Ah fuck," Aiden said. "When all those agencies get together and *coordinate*, sounds like a cluster fuck waiting to happen."

Jack didn't care. Well, he did. There were humans in the container being lowered. Of course he cared. But at this very moment, the team should be arriving in Rallos. He wanted to know Beth was safe. He prayed he'd get the call soon before he was called to where the rest of the *Hacha's* were gathered.

"It's going to be fine," Aiden assured him. "You know Mason and his team are the best out there."

Jack smiled faintly. "Apparently Beth is pretty damn good too." Lydia explained how Beth escaped with three other girls through a hole in the bottom of the train car. God, she was fucking amazing.

"JJ, Aiden, come here," Ruiz yelled out.

"Aiden, we need you to speak Chinese. It makes it easier if we have someone who can speak the language. We usually have to wait 'til we get to Mexico City, but since you're here, we can start now. Get into the container and calm their asses down. Tell them to do what we tell them. Tell them if they do, they get to come out, use a toilet, and get a warm meal, and if they fuck up, we'll kill them."

One of the *Hacha's* used bolt cutters to cut the chain and open the door. "Just hop on in there. We're driving into the city. We'll let you all out when we get there."

301

The door opened with a loud groan, and a huge waft of hot air and stink hit everyone. There was silence.

"Hey you in there. Say something," Ruiz shouted into the darkness. There was no reply.

"Hello," he shouted again. Still no response.

"Say something in Chinese," he demanded of Aiden.

Aiden yelled some Chinese into the mouth of the container. Still no reply.

"Oh fuck," Ruiz muttered. "Manuelo, get in there and check on them."

"I don't want to," the man whined.

"Shut up and do it." The man hoisted himself up and went in. He was in for about five minutes and came back out.

"Three of them are dead. There's two others who are really sick."

"Goddammit. That's the second time it's happened. *El Cuchilla* is not going to be happy. Aiden, get in there and talk to them. We'll see if it's worth trying to repair them."

Repair?! Where the fuck was the DEA? The DHS? If they didn't get here in the next three minutes, Jack was going to start shooting and asking questions later. He could see by the look in Aiden's eye he'd be on board with that plan.

Sirens screamed.

Lights blinded.

"You're under arrest," someone yelled over a bullhorn.

"Hands where we can see them."

Jack dropped his gun and raised his hands. Aiden did the same thing.

****

"Dammit." The truck came to an abrupt halt.

Beth moaned. Everything hurt.

"It's going to be okay, there's just a fallen tree. The men are moving it so they can keep driving."

"That doesn't sound like everything is okay." They'd been driving for over an hour. The main man who'd arrested her told her there was a reward if she was taken to Veracruz. Somebody named *El Cuchilla* wanted her. Beth would bet anything Berto had taken a new name.

"We're going to be sold," Missy sobbed.

"At least, we're not going to be killed," Joanne snapped.

"Death would be better."

303

Beth struggled to sit up.

"Stay where you are." Joanne gently pushed her back into her lap.

"No, I need to get up. Lying down is making me carsick." Joanne let her up. She felt the first plop of rain hit her head.

"Oh my God, is it raining?" Missy wailed.

"Would you shut the fuck up?" Joanne yelled.

"Silence," one of the two guards said.

The other guard must have heard something because he looked over the side of the truck, and then went over head first. The guard who told them to be quiet went to check what happened, and he too went over the side of the truck.

Missy cried out when she saw a dirt covered face peer over the side.

"Shut up, Missy!" Beth said in a loud whisper. "All of you be quiet. He's a friend."

Drake pulled himself over the side.

"Are you all okay?" Drake asked.

"We're fine," Beth assured him. He looked her over.

"You look like shit, Beth. But we have to move fast." A gunshot rang out. "Get down, now!" All four women hit the floor of the truck bed. Drake rested on top of Beth, his gun in his hand.

"Drake, we're clear. How are the women?" It sounded like Mason talking.

"Beth's injured, the others look okay."

"How bad?" Definitely Clint's voice.

Drake was pulled off her, and Clint pulled her into his arms. "Oh baby, look at you." Tears glistened in his eyes. "Dare, get over here. She's got to be in pain. You need to look at her. Her cheek could be broken."

"I'm fine, Clint. Don't worry."

"I'll worry all I want." Clint's fingers gently brushed her cheek.

"Where's Jack?"

"He's in Veracruz. He's been driving himself crazy looking for you. There are a bunch of women coming in from overseas he's helping. If I have to guess, Berto doesn't have much longer on this Earth."

"How did you find us?" Joanne wanted to know.

"A little kid named Jorge told us which way you went."

"Who are you?" Missy asked.

"I'm going to be her brother-in-law," Clint answered. "Darius, what's keeping you?" They heard two more gunshots.

"I'll be right there. I was busy." Beth laughed as she saw Joanne's eyes widen.

****

"We haven't found him." Jack looked at the man in the windbreaker with DHS emblazoned on the back. "But we've got the *Hacha's* gathered up."

"Do you have any idea where Guzman might be? Or Helen Martinez?"

"Nope."

Jack noted two of the mercs were gone too.

"If you think of anything, let us know."

"I will." He walked with Aiden towards the truck they'd been using since arriving in Veracruz.

"You know where he is, don't you?" Aiden asked.

"I have a damn good idea. Helen let it slip today when he lost his shit at the train station."

"Well, are you going to tell me or keep me in suspense?" Aiden asked as he got into the passenger seat.

"There's a small airport about ten miles north of the city. If the operation turned from sugar to shit, it was his escape hatch. Helen said he had a plane."

"Let's get on it."

"We can take it slow, you know he's going to make one more pass at Beth," Jack said grimly. He threw his cell phone at Aiden. "Get Lydia on the phone, I want a report."

Aiden dialed and put Lydia on speaker.

"Did they get her?"

"It's complicated."

"Did. They. Get. Her?" Jack demanded.

"I need fifteen more minutes."

"What the fuck, Lydia. They should have had her an hour ago," Jack ground out.

"It got complicated. The police arrested her. The guys went out after her. Last I heard they had her in their sights and she was alive and well. They were just going to recapture her and needed a half hour. That was fifteen minutes ago."

"I'm staying on the line."

"Gotchya."

Aiden had his phone out, and they followed the GPS coordinates to the airfield.

After twenty minutes, there was clicking on Jack's phone.

"Jack?" It was Beth.

"Beth! Oh my God, are you all right?"

"I'm fine." She giggled.

"Baby. I love you so much." It was the thing he most needed to say.

She laughed, such a carefree sound. "I love you this much."

"Dude, she has her arms spread really wide, and Darius had to hold her to stop her from falling over. She's pumped up with some really good drugs."

"Drake, why is she pumped up with drugs?"

"She's really hurting. It could be her cheekbone is cracked. Her hand is cut and needs stitches. She's got a massive bruise on her hip."

"I love you, Jack!" He heard her yell.

His breath hitched.

"I think she loves you," Aiden chuckled.

"We're driving to Mexico City. It's the safest place for her, and then we're taking a plane to San Diego," Mason said.

"Wanna see Jack."

"We have to get the girls stateside, Beth." There was a pause.

"Okay."

"Come home, Jack. I love you bunches."

"I have an errand, and then I'll be home."

****

They pulled up to the hangar that housed small planes, outside was a Lear jet. Jack spotted the Range Rover Helen used. He also recognized the missing mercenaries who were holding AK47's.

Aiden and Jack got out of their SUV.

The blonde haired mercenary tipped his chin.

"You got away. What about the others?"

"It was a total loss. We figured we would report. Is the boss inside?" Jack asked.

"Yeah. Let me tell him you're here, JJ. He doesn't want any surprises."

"Makes sense."

The man went inside. Aiden and Jack looked at one another. Aiden got up close to the other man.

"You got a cigarette?" The man shoved aside his rifle and put his hand in the pocket of his vest. Aiden, slipped out his knife, cut his throat, and eased him to the ground. Jack looked into the small side window and saw Helen, Berto, and the merc talking to each other with another man standing nearby. He was unarmed, and Jack assumed he was the pilot.

He held up four fingers. Aiden nodded.

The blonde mercenary came out, and before he could look around Jack had him by the throat, and broke his neck. He, too, slipped to the ground.

Jack and Aiden walked into the hangar.

"JJ! Aiden! Tell us everything." Helen rushed over to Aiden.

"DHS and DEA shut down your operation."

"Don't you mean our operation?" Berto asked.

"Sure, our operation," Jack corrected.

"Good, I need your help. The police said they would be here in less than an hour with the shipment we can take with us."

"You mean the girl you've been waiting for all this time, don't you, Berto?" Helen purred. She continued to stroke Aiden's chest despite his obvious distaste.

"She's one of the four. The other three will make us a lot of money. Don't worry Helen, we'll make out just fine. Also, Mr. Liu will still want to do business with us. Our operation in Cardenas hasn't been compromised."

"I disagree, I think she should be part of our merchandise," Helen said. She pushed away from Aiden and pulled out a gun. "You've gotten soft, Berto. This girl has made you crazy."

Jack looked from one to the other. *Crazy and evil if you asked him.* "JJ and Aiden will prefer working for the one who can give them the most profit, and that will be me. Mr. Liu has been talking to me on the side. He knows I have what it takes to help his distribution much more than you can."

Berto looked at Helen like he was seeing her for the first time.

"Aiden, get Berto's gun."

"Allow me," Jack said and sauntered over to Berto. He pulled out his K-Bar, and before Helen or Berto knew what was happening had the satisfaction of

311

stabbing Berto in the heart. Then he whispered in Berto's ear.

"That's for Beth, you sick fuck." Berto stared at him in horror as his eyes were slowly going blank.

"You just can't help taking out the trash, can you JJ?" Helen said in admiration.

"I guess not."

"Still too humanely, if you ask me. It must be the Eagle Scout shit." Aiden took aim and shot Berto in his dick, and the man let out a shrill shriek. Jack watched in satisfaction as blood poured from both wounds, and Berto breathed his last breath.

Aiden turned back to Helen. "Come here, beautiful," he coaxed.

She lowered her gun and went to him. He yanked her arm up behind her back with bruising force, and she smiled.

"At last, the way I like it."

"I'm glad you like it. We'll see what the DHS has in store for you, you crazy bitch."

Jack heard the jet take off.

****

"Where is she?"

"Calm down," Lydia soothed as she pulled him into a hug. He'd come bounding down the stairs into the baggage claim area and didn't see Beth.

"Is she okay?" He looked over Lydia's head where Clint grinned at him.

"Look, Darius gave her some pain pills. She was really hurting, but she wouldn't admit it. She's sleeping at our house. She's going to be pissed as hell she wasn't here to meet you, but she needed more rest."

Jack heaved a sigh. She was okay. He gave Lydia the hug she deserved.

"You did the right thing. Let's go, I need to see her."

"Mason has the car circling outside so you wouldn't have to wait," Clint said.

Another sigh of relief. Jack couldn't get to her fast enough.

Mason pulled up to the duplex in less than a half hour. Darius was waiting for them, and he looked stressed.

"What's wrong?"

"Later," he whispered.

"No, now," Jack demanded.

"It's nothing to do with Beth," he assured Jack. "She's in the back bedroom." He gave Darius a long look, and then continued down the hall when he heard Darius talking to Lydia and Clint. It was something about Rylie actually meeting with Mr. Liu in Vancouver, British Columbia, and Darius going bat shit crazy. Jack didn't give a fuck.

He opened the door.

Afternoon sunlight streamed into the room making it easy to see her swollen face. She'd kicked off the covers, and her sleep shirt was tugged up so he could see the beginnings of a bruise on her thigh. She looked like she'd been through a war. Tiny. Brave. His hero. She'd saved the lives of those girls. She twisted and rolled to the side. He knelt down at the side of the bed and stroked her hair from her face so he could inspect it closer. She smiled in her sleep.

"Jack," she murmured.

"Yes, sweetheart, it's me."

"I'm not high anymore. You're pretty. Will we have pretty babies?"

He couldn't breathe past the knot in his throat. He swallowed.

"Sweetheart. I think you're a little high, and yes, we're going to have gorgeous babies."

"Come lay with me." She grabbed the front of his T-shirt and tried to pull him into the bed with her. She winced. He gently grasped her hands and kissed the palm where she had the bandage.

"How many stitches, Beth?"

"A lot?"

"How many?"

"Ten."

Jack squeezed his eyes shut, but they still filled with tears.

"They told me what you did. You were amazing."

"Every minute. Every second, you were with me."

"I wanted to be."

"You killed Berto, didn't you?"

"He's dead, Beth. He'll never touch you, he'll never come after you again." He rested his forehead against hers, and she sighed in relief.

"Please hold me."

"Always."

Epilogue

"I got wet. I guess I'll have to get out of this dress soon," she said as she walked into the suite. She looked over her shoulder at Jack and loved the look on his face. The Bellagio fountains had only sprayed a little water on her, but seeing the avarice in his eyes when she suggested she strip, was exhilarating.

"I should help you," he choked out.

"Soon." She smiled. She sat down on the sumptuous sofa in the suite and crossed her legs, loving how his eyes followed her every move. He sat down next to her and rested his hand on her knee, caressing, tempting.

"I talked to Lydia."

"Let me guess, it was while I was on the phone with Aiden."

"We really need to turn off our cell phones."

"We did last night," he reminded her. Her entire body flushed at the memory.

"Anyway, I talked to Lydia, and she told me she hasn't been able to get ahold of Rylie since she went to Vancouver."

"Rylie goes off the reservation all the time."

"This time it's different. She feels it." Beth bit her lip.

"What else?"

"Your mom called Lydia, and she invited my whole family to the ranch." Jack nodded.

"I knew she was going to do that."

"But you don't like my father," Beth protested.

"You love your father, and he did the right thing. That's what matters. We're all going to have a great time at the ranch. My mom can't wait to meet everyone." Beth loved the idea.

"What about Aiden? What did he say?"

"Aiden can wait. I think getting you out of this dress is more important." He knelt in front of her and slipped the strappy sandals off her feet. Then he stood up and held out his hand to help her up. Jack placed a kiss under her jaw, and she shivered, then she lightly pushed him away so she could start towards the bedroom.

As she made her way to the double doors, she pushed the left strap of her white dress off her shoulder. She could feel Jack's eyes on her, and then she pushed off the right strap. She held the dress to her bosom until she was at the bed, then she let go. The dress fell to the floor.

"Oh God, you're wearing a thong," he groaned. She looked over her shoulder again and gave him the wickedest smile she had in her repertoire. It really wasn't all that wicked, but it felt so good to feel so free, and cherished, and try her hand at seduction. Jack's arms came around her, and her head fell against him. He tipped her chin and kissed her.

"Do you want to make love?"

"Yes," she said turning into his arms.

"Thank God," he said as he brushed the strap of her bra off her shoulder and cupped her breast. Beth moaned. Jack placed her gently on the bed. He knew she loved it when he did that.

"Thank you."

"For what?" he asked perplexed.

"For doing what I like."

"Thank you for this pretty white thong."

His big hand swept down her side to the curve of her waist, and then he slowly pulled off her panties. He stared at her, and she relished the look in his eyes. He found her beautiful. Wasn't it a miracle?

He took off his clothes, and she delighted in every inch of skin as it was revealed. Then his briefs came off, and all the air was sucked out of the room. She reached for him, and he slid down on top of her resting most of his weight on his arms.

"No, I need to feel you."

"You will." He kissed the side of her mouth, and she turned her head to capture his lips. Perfection.

Languid kiss after kiss, their hands stroking one another. Sighs filled the room. Beth slowly parted her legs, and cradled his hips. He kissed the bottom of her jaw and continued further. His lips sucking sweetly on one engorged nipple as his fingers lightly pinched the other tip. She cried out in pleasure, loving his caresses.

She was so needy for him, she pressed up, her folds wet, but he rolled away and reached over the side of the bed for protection. She grabbed at his arm.

"No!"

She caught the bright glitter of his blue eyes.

"Beth?"

"I want it all. I want a dirty house I get to clean. I want kids I get to raise. I want a man I get to love for the rest of my life."

"I want to be that man." His eyes shone as he came to rest on top of her. She arched up as he plunged deep.

"We belong to each other."

"Forever, sweetheart, we belong to each other, forever," he promised as he took her to the stars.

The End

If you enjoyed this book or any book, please consider leaving a review. It's appreciated by authors more than you know. Thank You! Caitlyn

Biography

Caitlyn O'Leary is an avid reader and considers herself a fan first and an author second. She reads a wide variety of genres but finds herself going back to happily-ever-afters. Getting a chance to write, after years in corporate America, is a dream come true. She hopes her stories provide the kind of entertainment and escape she has found from some of her favorite authors.

Keep up with Caitlyn O'Leary:

Facebook: http://tinyurl.com/nuhvey2

Twitter: http://twitter.com/CaitlynOLearyNA

Pinterest: http://tinyurl.com/q36uohc

Goodreads: http://tinyurl.com/nqy66h7

Website: http://www.caitlynoleary.com

Email: caitlyn@caitlynoleary.com

Books by Caitlyn O'Leary

The Found Series

Revealed, Book One

Forsaken, Book Two

Healed, Book Three

Midnight Delta Series

Her Vigilant SEAL, Book One

Her Loyal SEAL, Book Two

Her Adoring SEAL, Book Three

SEALED with a Kiss, Book Four *Free Novella*

Her Daring SEAL, Book Five

Fate Harbor Series Published by Siren/Bookstrand

Trusting Chance, Book One

Protecting Olivia, Book Two

Claiming Kara, Book Three

Isabella's Submission, Book Four

Cherishing Brianna, Book Five

34583734R00182

Made in the USA
San Bernardino, CA
01 June 2016